MICHÈLE OLSON

Being Ethel
(In a world that loves Lucy)

Library of Congress Control Number: 2019919845

Being Ethel (In a world that loves Lucy)

© 2020 by Michèle Olson. All rights reserved.

Published by Lake Girl Publishing

Green Bay, WI

www.LakeGirlPublishing.com

info@LakeGirlPublishing.com

First edition

ISBN: 978-1-7343628-0-0

This book was professionally typeset on Reedsy.
Find out more at reedsy.com

Acknowledgement

Being Ethel
(In a world that loves Lucy)

Cover design by Karen Kalbacher

Round Island Lighthouse painting by Michèle Olson

Interior layout by Raymond A. Olson II

First Edition: January 2020, printed in the U.S.A.

Dedication

To my husband, Raymond, who smiles at all my quirky and crazy endeavors, and this one has been a doozy! Thank you for your encouragement and love while I chase dreams. Mackinac Island and the Grand Hotel has been our special place for such a long time, why I could write with such insight. I love our time there and I love you!

To my children, Benjamin and Molly and their spouses, Cassie and Danny. You are my heart, my inner circle of family, ready to love and support me. To our grand babies from the "P" family, Jett and Jace – you are pure joy and light. This Gee Gee treasures every moment with you. Just thinking of you makes my heart leap with happiness. To my Australian sister from another mother, Cheryl-my heart sister. I love you all to the moon and back.

To Maxine R., your prayers and encouragement kept me going when I wasn't sure I could ever finish. You are a treasured friend.

To all my dear friends who were excited to see me write this novel, you know who you all are!

To J.J. whose wisdom helped me finally finish a book! And to my kindred author friends who offer endless encouragement in all things writing and publishing. We are doing it!

To Libby Sternberg, who gave me the perfect balance as an editor.

To Karen Kalbacher, who made the art and cover beautiful and what

I hoped for.

To Cris E., for jumping in with enthusiasm and fortitude. You made the website happen!

To those loved ones who left too soon, especially my heartbeats – my sister Mina, and my son Joel. An ultimately, to my reason to write and love – The Father, The Son, and The Holy Spirit.

And finally, to you dear reader. I never thought I would get here, a published book. I hope it brings you joy. Keep chasing your dreams and keep your eyes on The One who provides each true need.

To Him, you are everything.

Jesus did many other things as well. If every one of them were written down, I suppose that even the whole world would not have room for the books that would be written.

John 21:25 New International Version (NIV)

Chapter One

1979

"Are you looking forward to sitting in a jail cell, young lady?"

If weasels spoke, this is what they would sound like. Lovely way to wake up, with my rent-a-lawyer screaming at me on the phone.

"You know I don't want that. I overslept. Geez, it happens," I say. All twenty-three-year-olds oversleep, for crying out loud. I'm still not convinced there is a five o'clock in the morning. Probably made up by an alarm clock company.

One of my many talents, getting my rent-a-lawyer to scream at me over the phone.

"I was able to get your hearing postponed until noon, but, Piper, I swear, if you don't show up this time, I'll recommend a maximum sentence myself. You got that?" Wham!

A person could break a phone slamming it that hard. Extra emphasis noted, Perry Mason. Thankfully, I have developed an antidote to crabby people, and it's as easy as pushing the play button on my cassette player. And, there we go. "Good Morning" with Debbie Reynolds, Gene Kelly, and Donald O'Connor blaring is what I always need to change a toxic atmosphere. I hope this helps. Yes, there's the beat and the rhythm that

1

gets me going. I'm right here with you gang, tap left, tap right, sway left, sway right. Wait. That extra beat, that's not me. Great, now I've got someone pounding on my door.

"Christopher Columbus, stop trying to knock down my door!" Good girl, Piper! You didn't swear! Yes, drawing on this line Jo uses in *Little Women* has helped with my potty mouth, if I do say so myself.

Phones. Doors. As Garbo said, "I want to be left alone." The pounding is messing with the cool vibe I have going.

I unlock the first lock, the second one, and the dead bolt. And, here it comes, CREEEK! That is a sound that crawls up my spine every time. And, what have we here? Hello scrawny teenager in your oversized, dark uniform shoving a paper at me. Shouldn't you be at the malt shop sipping milk shakes?

"Finally! Sign here and then I can give you the telegram," he says.

Not a blasted telegram, not on this day. And, where are they getting telegram people lately? Are you twelve yet, Skippy?

"Hey, Pip, see you're getting a telegram, that's so weird, today of all days. Is the coffee ready yet?" Freddy, my neighbor from across the hall, steps out of his apartment. I don't think he's owned a razor since 1962 or thought about new clothes since then. Do a striped shirt and plaid pants ever work together?

Crap! Why do I always forget Freddy day? And, yes. He's been cooking cabbage again. Skippy's face tells the whole story of what it smells like to get to close to Freddy's apartment.

"You're a loud knocker, sonny boy, made the plates rattle in my place," Freddy says.

"Hang on, Sk... sir... mister." I don't know what to call this nerd kid.

To my neighbor, I say, "Yah, about that, Freddy, today may not be a good day for coffee."

"What you sayin', Pip? Speak up!" Freddy is already in my kitchen alcove and I hear the tin spoon hitting the side of the pot as he's probably

2

putting the grounds in the bottom, not the cartridge on top.

"Can you sign? I've got other deliveries. Wow, someone likes cabbage around here. Just sign, and then I can give it to you, ma'am."

'Ma'am'. I'm way too young to be a ma'am, but maybe I look old because you look like your mom still tucks you in. You can lose the attitude, Skippy.

"Cabbage is a staple here at our De La Subsidized Villa—no Rockefellers here, buddy boy." I say. "You got a pen? It would take me a while to find one."

Ironic that pens elude me when my last name is Penn.

"Of course, I carry a pen because no one ever has one. People are…"

"People are busy and not expecting a door-pounding, ever think of that?" I say. Grouch at me and I'll grouch back at you.

A loop and some scribbles are close enough. Geez, Skippy, stare much? Take a picture why you're at it. Oh yah, he thinks he deserves a tip.

"Freddy! Got a dollar for a tip?" Freddy always has money in his crusty pockets, along with a few buttons, paperclips, and gum wrappers. Sure, Freddy, you darn near knock me over getting into the kitchen, but feel free to take your sweet time to get me the buck.

"Used to be cheaper to send a telegram than make a long-distance call when I was a kid." Freddy just has to speak with every shuffling step.

"Give him the dollar, Freddy." Can this little ensemble of weirdos hear my jaw clenching?

It feels good to slam the door in snarky telegram boy's face. And, score. I have a new pen.

"In fact, I read…" Oh boy, Freddy-Know-It-All has something he thinks only he knows.

"People used the word *stop* at the end of a sentence 'cuz punctuation cost extra, but the word *stop* was free. So, their telegram was cheaper in the long run. Bet you didn't know that!" Freddy says.

"When did you become the 1979 king of all things telegram?"

"Pip, have you looked in a mirror today?"

"Yeah, I'm Miss America," I say. I too had the misfortune of catching a glimpse of myself in the hall mirror as I headed to the door. That last attempt at cutting my own hair was not a good idea in hindsight. Thin, blonde hair has a mind of its own if you don't wash and style it every day, and who has that kind of time? What's so bad about bib overalls and a T-shirt? Faded doesn't always mean worn out, does it? I bet if Twiggy wore it, the fashion mags would be all over it.

"I'll pay back that buck, Freddy, after I get to a bank sometime."

I won't be paying him back. I ask for a dollar here and there, and Freddy hands it over. It's just what we do.

"A telegram, arriving today and on the exact same day. When I woke up, I saw my mark on my bank calendar. I put a little star there 'cuz I know what it means. Four whole years since that other one, and then you get one today? It's weirding me out," Freddy says.

"Well, the last thing we need is more weirdness out of you, and I have no idea who it's from. It's probably nothing, and I don't have time to read it now. I've got to be downtown, and the BART is busy on Fridays—so let's rain check on our coffee and gossip date, do you mind?"

"That goofy subway. There's walking and cable cars. Kids today. I only came by 'cuz it's Friday, and Friday 9 a.m. is when I always come by. Do you own a watch, Pip? I've lived through riots and 'Nam and darn near the Depression. I can live without your crappy coffee. And quit playing your music so loud!"

Great, now I've hurt his feelings. Apparently, this stupid get-together has become important to the Fredster.

"Freddy…" Maybe I can salvage this horrible morning for him at least. "Although you weren't on the front lines in Vietnam, your honorable

4

service as the best guard who ever worked at Alcatraz is appreciated by the proud citizens of San Francisco. Sunday we'll have time to talk before the *I Love Lucy* show starts. I'll even treat you to a sandwich afterward. But, today, I have this appointment and I can't miss it, or it will be really bad."

"Secrets… appointments… telegrams… all right. I didn't get to be seventy-five next birthday and this handsome by not being able to take a hint," Freddy says. "What did you do, rob a bank?"

You're not far off, Freddy. At least my deal gets him going toward the door.

"I miss them too," Freddy says. "Best neighbors I ever had in this crap hole. Your dad always asked how I was, at least until he got on TV. And, your mom made me muffins sometimes. Your sister was always laughing and smiling. I couldn't tell you apart when you were little. *Now, those twins are identical* I always said to the Mrs. Then you talked, and I knew which one you were. Sassy, sassy, sassy. That's what I used to say to the Mrs. when she was still here. *That one is sassy.*"

"Ironic, huh, Freddy? You liked all of them the best and you're stuck with me. God is playing a joke on you."

Four more shuffles. Come on Fred-meister, you can do it. Keep going.

"Pip, I know it's a tender day." Freddy's face softens.

"Freddy, tick-tock! Let me get the door."

I can't do this right now. Even the watch I don't own is ticking loudly in my head.

"Don't you think it's draftier in here every year? Wow, Pip, ever think about oiling this door?"

"Okay, well… see you Sunday for *I Love Lucy*." Hopefully this push cleverly disguised as a pat gets him out the door and saves me from another Freddy knowledge-fest.

"I'm going, I'm going. It wouldn't hurt to throw a few cookies on the table along with the crappy coffee you get. No one likes a bad hostess, I always say."

"Well, just bring a note from your doctor saying that Fredrick J. Coleman has permission to eat cookies even though he has diabetes and needs to stay away from sugar."

"Sassy, sassy, sassy…" Freddy always had to have the last word.

I don't dare look at his face again. I can't take what I know is there, someone who knows and cares. Freddy, there's no time for this, no time for tears.

"I know what the day means, I know." His voice breaks.

Nope. I can't do feelings and things today.

"On your way, Sir Fredrick of Fredrickville… life goes on." I give a bow and a hand flourish, hoping I can get a smile back. Nope. Didn't work. Sorry, King of the Telegrams. You don't understand. And, the reality of what could be ahead makes me crazy afraid to find out for myself.

Chapter Two

A telegram from Michigan. My only Michigan connection is Trixie, and heaven knows we haven't talked in years. We thought we would be in touch every day after the summer I lived with her and her great aunt. That's how thirteen-year-olds think. I'll never forget that summer. It was one of the best times of my life. Besides, it's 1979 not 1939, for Pete's sake. No one from my generation would send a telegram. This whole day is giving me a stomachache. I feel like Barbara Stanwyck in *Titanic,* about to hit the iceberg. "Enough, Piper—open the freakin' telegram!" Great. Now I'm talking to myself, out loud, on subways.

And here come the stares. Sorry, Mr. Gray Hair with the bow tie. You shouldn't have sat so close to me. He's probably English and knows the Queen. I bet he never takes the BART, but today his car is in the garage and he gave the chauffeur the day off. Yes, I'm sorry I interrupted your reading of Charles Dickens and I know that look. You think I'm a subway crazy, the ones who talk out loud to imaginary rabbits, which, according to Jimmy Stewart, are not so invisible as you think. I should have opened the dumb thing before I left. This stupid court date is making me nuts. Deep breaths. Mom always said, deep breaths. Rip the bandage off now, or I'll have to wait until after court. What if I go straight to jail and they take my satchel away, and I never see inside the telegram? Amazing how a crummy piece of paper can change your whole life. Here goes nothing.

Theresa Masters from Mackinac Island, Michigan, deceased from natural causes STOP You are named as sole heir of her store and residence on the island STOP To understand the monetary value and how to secure inheritance please appear at law offices of Stumpf & Sawyer no later than May 25, 1979 STOP Failure to do so will forfeit your inheritance to Mackinac City Council for determination of next steps STOP

What? Theresa... my Trixie! We haven't talked in forever, but this news hurts. Trixie, when you let me stay with you that summer on the island, you saved me from schlepping around the country in a missionary dog and pony show. Who wants to spend their summer raising missionary funds with parents and a Goody Two-shoes twin sister? Instead of buying into the whole evangelism shtick—sitting on hard pews in musty buildings listening to endless sermons and off-key singers while they raised funds—I had a glorious summer with you, my sweet pen pal. That school pen-pal project saved me right when I needed a change. To this day I'm shocked my parents gave their blessing. Whatever your aunt said on that phone call made it possible. My dad paying for long distance was a miracle, too. Man, what a place. Mackinac Island, as close to paradise as I could imagine. Blood sisters, we had vowed, kind of strange when you have a twin. Hormones and boys. That's what caused us to lose touch. Now you're dead, only twenty-three—just like me. How do you die of natural causes so young? Why would you leave me your stuff? Your aunt must be gone by now, and you never talked about any other relatives. Still, there must be someone better than me. How am I going to get to Mackinac Island by May 25th? Or, will I be in jail? Ugh, my BART stop. I can't think about this right now. At least the guy sitting by me can stop worrying if he's in harm's way from a subway crazy. I didn't say any of that out loud, I hope. Enjoy your date with Miss Havisham, sir, and give my best to the Queen.

* * *

Surreal, scary, and not pretty, but somehow, the judge didn't see me as complete scum.

It felt like I was floating in a daydream, even as he was pounding that gavel. So much pounding today, including my heart and head. I think there might have been a bit of yelling in his voice when he told me to pay the fine or I would do the jail time. He did remind me of the judge in *Miracle on 34th Street* when they were trying Kris Kringle and all the letters show up on his bench from the kids who wrote to Santa Claus. He must have seen something he liked, or it was a pity move. Maybe he was just busy and wanted me gone. At any rate, I'm not going to jail!

"You understand this is unheard of. This judge always gives jail time. Did you get that, loud and clear, that if you ever shoplift again, there will be no second chances?"

I feel little flicks of spit hitting my face as the weasel and his voice are way too close for my liking. Yes, rent-a-lawyer, I get it. I also get you seem disappointed I'm not going to jail.

"That hearing went far better than I hoped for in my wildest dreams, not that you deserved such a lenient sentence. If there's a brain in your head, you will pay the fine on time, and you will never, ever shoplift again. If you don't believe in God, this is the time to start, because what just happened, Piper... that was a miracle. So, say your prayers, Miss Lucky, because multiple offenses never get off that easy. Take a hint and don't shoplift ever again. I don't mean not get caught, I mean never do it. And if you do decide to do it again, don't call me."

"Thank you!" I probably should have said that a little quicker because I doubt he heard it halfway down the block when I finally was able to speak and wipe off my face. I get it, you don't like your job. No need to take it out on me, rent-a-lawyer.

"Eh, be gone, before someone drops a house on you, too." That's all that comes to mind right now. Public defenders need personality lessons. They get stuck with cases they don't want. Maybe things went well because God owes me one. I wasn't ready to be an orphan. It's probably not how it works, but we all keep score. I don't care. He was no prize as a lawyer, no Katharine Hepburn or Spencer Tracy in *Adam's Rib*. With them on board, I would have ended up with scads of money and living happily ever after. That's how Hollywood does things, always a satisfying ending, always getting it right. Hollywood never lets me down. I hate this day, but I'll still take it over this day four years ago when the first blasted telegram showed up.

It was Walter Cronkite who informed the country on the evening news that my whole family had died. Either indigenous people burning down a hut with a TV evangelist, his wife, and his daughter inside is a big story, or it was a slow news day. No state department representative pounded on my door that day—hut-burning protocols were probably not in the training manual at the agency. I didn't see Walter say it. I was sitting in a corner with the lights out in my apartment like paralyzed roadkill. It was the first telegram I ever received. When the guy brought it, I thought I had won something, like some movie scene. Talk about stupid. After the numbness wore off, all I felt was anger. *Teen Beat Magazine* had an article saying there were different stages of grief. I read it. I feel one stage all day, every day—anger—a fancy word for mad, mad, mad! As if they can sum up devastation in a two-page spread, all wrapped in a neat "How to Become Alive Again" package. And, those comments at the funeral were no help.

"Aren't you happy? They are with the angels now."

"I know exactly how you feel, my aunt just died, and she was ninety-seven, bless her heart."

"Now you have three guardian angels to watch over you."

"It was God's will."

My favorite comment was from a hippie guy who said he watched my dad on TV once. All he said was: "Well, that's a crappy thing to happen."

Preach it, brother. So, now, my pocket has a fresh new telegram. Like four years ago, a yellow piece of paper is breaking my heart and changing my life. And once again, I don't know what to do.

Right now, I need some kind of "Get-Out-of-Jail-Free" card celebration. If Trixie were here, she would have celebrated with me. She was the one who introduced me to my first five-finger escapade, but her goals didn't go beyond bubble gum and lip gloss. Funny she ended up being a store owner on Mackinac Island.

This fine will wipe the final stash under my mattress so this party must be cheap. That's it—Frap! Yeah, it pays to be friends with the ticket booth guy at the Bijou. Frap lets me waltz right in, no trying to sneak in the side door. Frap and I don't care about real life stuff… we live for old movies. It's like an unwritten rule—don't spoil life as it should be with reality. Thank goodness my mom taught me to always put a dime in my shoe. The next phone booth will be my ticket to an evening of escape. And fiddle-dee-dee, I'll think about my problems tomorrow.

"Hello, The Bijou, can I help you?"

"Hey, Frap, it's Piper… I'm in need of a movie!"

"Miss P, it's been too long!" Frap is a hoot. "Up for some *Singin' in the Rain?*"

"Are you kidding me? I was just enjoying some 'Good Morning' earlier today."

"Ah, the trio can't wait to hang out! The movie starts in two hours and I'm ready for my break—wanna catch a burger?" Frap asks.

Frap's a mind reader! I don't remember eating today; a hamburger sounds amazing. Maybe that's why I was so spacey in court.

"Frap, you're a lifesaver. I'm starving and ready for some love from the big screen. I'll catch the BART and be at Jack-in-the-Box in ten or fifteen."

"Sounds like a plan… hey, did you get together with your cousin?"

"My cousin? I don't have a cousin. Tell me at dinner, I gotta catch the BART."

Cousin? Frap's been eating the brownies. Why is someone asking about me and why are they asking Frap? I keep my "Frap-life" very separate from the rest of my glowing existence. People asking about me. Who am I in trouble with now?

Chapter Three

"Kinda' strange you called me today, because I wanted to remember to tell you about this cousin thing," Frap says.

The smell of the burgers is making me salivate.

"We did say the works, didn't we, on the burgers? It's a sin to eat a burger without the works, don't you think, Frap?"

"It's all cool, Piper, we said the works. Now, what about this cousin of yours?"

"That word's not even in my vocabulary. Frap, you don't know much about me, but you do know about my family's deaths, there's no cousins. My parents were only children."

"I knew your family met the grim reaper, but I figured there could be a cousin or two. It was this lady and guy trying to find out where you worked, but I don't even know the answer to that, so probably a good thing. I told her we're movie buddies and then I felt a little funny and clammed up. I should have been more suspicious. But, don't worry, I didn't really tell them anything except how much you love old movies 'cuz I thought they were your relation and into movies too. You think I screwed up?"

"No, it's okay. You didn't know. We mind our own beeswax and I like that about us. Wouldn't it have been easier for them to find out where I live and ask me or… unless… Freddy," I say.

"The Fredster Astaire! How is the old dude? I remember when you brought him to see *The Long, Long Trailer* with Lucy and Ricky. Man, he couldn't stop talking about how much he loved that duo," Frap says.

"They must have been looking for me, and Freddy told them I come here sometimes. That must be it. But saying they were my cousins—that's weird. Frap, I'm sorry you were subjected to my insanity. I am gonna yell at Fred Flinstonian and ask him not to tell strangers my business. He probably thought he was helping, and heaven knows he loves an audience. Thanks for clamming up when you did. I've had a little trouble with the powers that be lately, so it could be social workers looking for some dirt or a reason to kick me out of housing. Anyway, Gene Kelly is saving me a seat, and oh good, our burgers. We should chow down and get to the Bijou," I say.

"Burgers it is and then you're right, I've got to get back too and get that ticket window open," Frap says.

"One other thing, Frap—you may not see me for a while after this. I'm making a trip and I don't know how long I'll be gone. I don't want you to think I died or something. There seems to be an awful lot of that going around lately."

"You are a lady of mystery. Sounds like a good movie plot! Like you said, Piper, we don't snoop in each other's stuff. It's just Hollywood and more Hollywood. But, if you do ever need the old Frap, I'm here for ya, like Mickey Rooney for Judy Garland. I do have something I was wondering but felt funny asking. I know you don't like talking about the past, but it must have been cool to see your dad treated like a star when he landed on TV, I mean I even saw him in the paper," Frap says.

"It's okay. Lots of people were starting to think my dad was cool, and it felt like he kept getting more famous because of being on TV so much."

I've gotta appease Frap, but I hate talking about my dad. I have just the tidbit that will trip his trigger.

"I think it was a lot for him to take in for a guy who started as a preacher in a tiny church," I say. "He was just starting to get famous, not enough to help us with a decent living yet, but he was headed that way. You will get a kick out of this, he met one of the Beatles. He met Ringo! They passed in a hall in a TV studio and talked for a minute."

"Wow! Ringo! That's so cool! We're showing *Hard Day's Night* next month. Let me know if you're back, I'll get you in!"

Good. Frap's curiosity seems satisfied.

"I'll take care of this check, Piper. Seems like you had a hard day instead of a *Hard Day's Night.*"

"Ah Frap, you're the best! I owe you one, like a million times now. Thanks, buddy."

I can't wait to get to the theater and escape into a perfect world of music and feel like their life is my life. I'm relieved I thought of something to tell Frap. If he knew the truth about my dad, he wouldn't be singing his praises—ever.

Chapter Four

Even the calming effect of *Singin' in the Rain* can't bring me down from the way my body is still buzzing. Lying in bed after this day, my brain won't let up. Frap's question got me thinking about my dad, which I hate doing. There are so many questions that will never get answered, and I'm tired of wondering if I could have changed anything. While my dad was telling people that God loved them, he was being a royal grouch and obnoxious to us. The hours before a service were tense and horrible, with everything being my mom's fault or my fault. It's quite a trip to see a person ooze love and acceptance in the pulpit yet act the way he did at our house. I'll never understand it or forgive him for it. The dough had just started to come, so it wasn't that. And, I don't think he cared about the money. From what I remember, he never set out to be a TV preacher. It just spiraled after a guest appearance on some big-name preacher's shows. The ratings went up and they came looking for him.

It was in my mother's diaries where I learned how he treated her. She hid it from us, and she did a good job because I was shocked by what she wrote. Absorbed in my own life, I wasn't paying attention. I guess there were a few signs. After a service, when lots of people had patted my dad on the back and told him what a great speaker he was, then it was all ice cream and taffy. As soon as she asked him anything or if he talked about it not going the way he wanted, it was time to walk on eggshells again. We never knew what might set him off. I heard him swear under his breath, but he didn't take the Lord's name in vain. I suppose there's points for that. Still, I wish I could have helped her with the pain she must have felt. The first time I read her diary, I had to smile about how she vented—writing to a different movie star in each of the entries. The one she wrote shortly before their last trip was hard to take.

Dear Ingrid Bergman,

I'm ready for a change. I know how you felt when you were so torn in your role in Casablanca—go with Victor or stay with Rick when the stakes were high. So many times, I've thought of leaving, prayed for the right answer. My faith is strong that something good will come out of all of this. I'm hoping the trip to Africa will change things, Thomas will calm down and return to his first love—Our Lord Jesus. The lure of TV makes him worse and now he's started on Piper too. I wish she would guard her tongue; it only makes it worse when we're alone. Ingrid, my self-worth comes from who I am to the Lord, not this man. It has to be that way, or I could never recover from the words he says. They are cruel, mean, hateful, and nothing a woman would want to hear from the person who is supposed to love her here on earth. When we go out to minister, I hide my hurt because I don't want to get in the way of the message that can change lives. I'm a praying person, Ingrid, and I'm asking the Lord that this upcoming trip to Africa will be a turning point in our marriage and our family. And, Ingrid, I love your movies. I hope you are doing well in your life. You've given me many moments of escape and fun.

A big fan,

Betty

Seeing her diaries is what made me write to movie stars in my diary. I wish my mom was here so I could talk to her and tell her I'm sorry for what she went through and for the part I played in making it worse. I wish I had a sleeping pill or something. Lying here isn't working. Maybe writing in my journal will be cathartic and then I can finally sleep. Worth a try.

Dear Marilyn,

You know what it feels like to have your life painted into a corner, to not know what to do next. I'm so sad about how you passed but I enjoy the gift you left in your movies. Right now, I wish I was in How to Marry a Millionaire, because if I was, I wouldn't be stuck where I am right now trying to decide if I go to Mackinac Island or stay here. If there's money for me on the island, that's where I need to head. At least here, so close to 1980, I don't have to marry a man to get out of my life situation like you did at sixteen. I bet you often wished life were much more like the movies than reality— scampering around with Tony Curtis and Jack Lemmon. You must have laughed so hard when making Some Like it Hot with them. The thing is, dear Marilyn, I don't have much to keep me here, including any job prospects. Trixie and I both loved your movies when we were junior-high age, and we talked and giggled far into the night when I lived on the island with her. We took turns trying on a wig that looked like your hair and putting on lots of red lipstick. You gave a lot of happiness to two awkward schoolgirls who dreamed anything in life was possible. Maybe you're hanging out with Trixie right now in that great theater in the sky! I would like to think so, anyway. Here's an idea, how's about I go to Mackinac, sell off the place fast, and do a little traveling? I could go to New York and become a vagabond. My parents used to call people 'bums' and 'hobos', but I like 'vagabond' or 'gypsy'. I could go to Greenwich Village and hang out at coffee shops. With my sketchbook and watercolors, I could be a street artist. Well, thanks for thinking this through with me, Marilyn. I guess I have no choice but to see this thing through, head to Mackinac Island, sell the place and go from there. Maybe I'll make enough to get myself a nice diamond necklace. As we both know... well, you get it. Thanks for the movies, Marilyn. Let's hope there's a happier ending for me in the weeks to come. This girl could use a break.

Your admirer,

Piper Penn

If anyone knew I did this... so silly. Mom, it makes me feel closer to you. I need to make checklists; they always help. That's what I need, order and organization. Checklist it is.

1. Convince Freddy that he can get my apartment sublet without letting the housing authority know about it.
2. Pay the fine. There goes all my money.
3. Become a scathingly brilliant but broke nomad, sell anything I can to get a plane ticket to Detroit, a bus ticket to Mackinaw City, and a ferry to Mackinac Island.
4. Try to hang onto my sanity while I'm getting all of this done.

Well, two out of three as they say. Time to go over the rainbow and take a chance. Okay Mackinac Island, please be good to me again.

Chapter Five

"You look a little lost, ma'am."

There it is, the sensation of a new wrinkle growing with another "ma'am." Ma'ams are at least forty, sir. But this guy putting his hand out to help me off the ferry is a perceptive fellow. I am lost.

"Oh, sorry, I'm not exactly sure where I'm going." I say.

That's putting it mildly. There I go again, in la-la land. It all started with the waves hitting the sides of the ferry. For a minute or two, I wasn't me in the now; I was me back then. The clip-clop of the horses as their hooves hit the pavement in perfect rhythm, the smell of sugar and chocolate as fudge is made for the day, the lilacs and the fragrant sweetness of those purple blossoms that lingers far after the season is over—everything that Mackinac Island is famous for is rushing back to me.

It's a far cry from stealing stuff in Chinatown in San Fran. Why does anyone have to grow up past thirteen? If I could have stayed that age, oh the garbage I could have escaped, so much crap. I would have lived in the perpetual "oh my gosh, he looked at me" phase, enough to keep me chipper and humming for days.

And Trixie. Why didn't you stay thirteen instead of growing up to die in your twenties, what's that about? I don't think there's enough fudge on this island to get me through life after that intoxicating age of perfection, minus the pimples. I wanna try to keep going. If I have to live through all life has thrown at me, it makes perfect sense to do it with unlimited fudge.

"Can I point you in a certain direction, ma'am?" the man asks.

Again, with the ma'am, and that's my new shoes stepping in the horse poo. Mr. Helpful is covering his mouth, probably trying to hide his big smile at what I did.

"Sorry, we're usually quicker at getting to that kind of thing, so that kind of thing doesn't happen to pretty little ladies like you."

This guy is talking like he's in a John Wayne movie. He must have missed the memo that Mackinac Island is in the Upper Peninsula of Michigan and not out west.

"Actually, sir, it matches up to my life lately."

"Oh, come on, now, little lady, you're on the island. Life is good here."

"Sorry, I don't want to spread my sour sunshine to such a helpful person. Can you point me to the law firm of Stumpf and Sawyer?"

"Oh, surely. Just cross Main Street straight ahead and take a left on the next street up. That's Market Street. It's halfway into the block, you can't miss it. It's next to a souvenir shop, in case you're looking for some trinkets to take home with you."

"Thank you. I'll just be sure and make a nice walk through the grass, so I don't spread this shoe frosting."

"Oh here, see this little piece of steel sticking up, that's what we call a poo scraper, at least when we're with a lady! Just scrape your shoe on that, and you'll not have a care in the world anymore." He gestures toward the steel.

Man, this guy is happier than, well, me in a fudge shop. Mister Rogers meets John Wayne comes to mind.

"Thanks again, you have been very helpful," I say.

"Not at all. You have yourself a nice day now. Remember, you're on the island now," he replies.

Yes, yes, I am on the island. May horse poo, lilac trees, and an abundance of fudge sprinkle on me and turn my life around. Who knows what lies ahead after what I'll hear at "Do We Cheat 'Em and How," as Freddy refers to all law firms? But I get it. This place is beautiful, and calming, and it feels like its own Shangri-La. Ah, my favorite director—Mr. Frank Capra and *Lost Horizon* from 1937. Yes, that's the vibe. Horses, people on regular bikes and those tandem bikes—forgot about them. Trixie and I loved to ride tandem, playing rock, paper, and scissors to see who had to take the front. I won the most.

Why is there a movie camera being loaded on a flatbed ready to be pulled by a team of horses? And more movie equipment, it looks like. People are pointing and staring. They must be making "Mackinac Island, The Movie." Good idea, really. Hollywood meets Mackinac Island. I like it. The big excursion it took for me to get here—now that's script-worthy. Planes, buses, boats, and now my future holds horses and bikes. But, I did it. I made it here, and once again I'm daydreaming so much that I don't remember the walk to this lawyer's front door. I hope turning the doorknob of this office opens a new beginning. A law office is not my favorite first stop, but here goes nothing. Please don't sound like a weasel!

"Hello, my name is Piper Penn, and I have an appointment with Mr. Sawyer." The receptionist has a nice smile. Such friendly islanders!

"Yes, we've been expecting you. Please have a seat and Mr. Sawyer will be right with you. Can I get you anything to drink?" she asks.

"No, I'm fine, thanks."

That's a lie. I'm dying of thirst and pretty much just dying, but never once have I seen a person in the movies accept an offer of water or coffee in a business meeting, and I get my education from the best—the

For Leigh

Does have a ~~women~~ faith based theme

ne-6,1-diyl)bis(2-hexyldecanoate),
ecylacetamide, 1,2-distearoyl-sn-glycero-3-

ay have been updated. For the most recent
visit https://dailymed.nlm.nih.gov/dailymed/.

ider or visit www.COMIRNATY.com or call

movies. I will stick with what I know. This girl is in control, if you overlook the horse poo remnants on my shoe.

"Miss Penn. Pleased to meet you, I'm William Sawyer. Won't you follow me into my office?"

A light handshake and the obligatory comment about the weather and let's do this. A young Jimmy Stewart in *Mr. Smith Goes to Washington*, that sums you up, Mr. Sawyer, but you do need to work on your voice. Not weaselly, thank goodness, but more like Kermit the Frog. Uh, I think you mean 'follow you into the rest of my life', Jimmy Frog. Take the money and run seems to be my best direction, and oh, Trixie, I don't want to disrespect your memory, but I hope you left me some money. Money would solve all my problems. With money I can take off and do and be whatever I want. It's like when Clarence, the angel in *It's a Wonderful Life*, tells Jimmy Stewart's character they don't use money in heaven. And, then my favorite line—Jimmy's character reminds him it comes in pretty handy down here! Money, sweet money. I would head to Hollywood. Yes, that would be my first stop—Grauman's Chinese Theatre.

"Miss Penn. I said this way into my office."

Oh man, I'm trying to be professional, and instead I'm acting like a space head.

"Sorry, I'm just tired from my long trip," I explained. I don't think I've apologized so much in my whole life as I have since I arrived here in Happy Horsey Land.

"Have a seat, and I am sorry for the loss of your friend. I didn't know her on a personal level, you understand. The founder of our firm did work for her great aunt at one point so that's probably why she picked us to be the executor of her will. She must have done the paperwork with him before I joined the firm. With her aunt gone and no living relatives, we had no idea she had a will. It's not typical for someone so young. It was found after her death in a safe deposit box at the bank, one of those things you research when someone passes."

"I was shocked to hear she passed. We haven't been in touch the last few years."

"I understand. Had there been no will, the property would have reverted to the town council and been put up for sale. It seems the money she inherited from her relative's estate was used to purchase this property from a gentlemen friend of her aunt."

This is all starting to feel too real. Could they open a window? It's so hot in here.

"Anyway, there are papers to go over and things to look at, but the bottom line is—she left you her little store on the corner of Main and Market Streets which also has a small apartment above it. You most likely passed it on your way here when you turned the corner."

"Today is a blur. I wasn't paying much attention to anything on the street, and just making sure I got to your office." I neglected to admit I remembered nothing past scraping the poo off my shoe.

"No problem, but I should warn you it hasn't been kept up. The store itself has been in a state of demise for the last few years. She barely had it open during the tourist season, so there are no real products to sell. You're not inheriting much in store inventory, but any property on the island is quite valuable, especially since so few properties are independently owned outside of the Sims-Dubois families. They are the founding families, so that stands to reason. Perhaps you might find more satisfaction by selling the property and getting back to your life in San Francisco after you fulfill the further stipulations of the will. If that interests you, I am fully prepared to work with the Sims-Dubois family representative to make sure they make you a generous offer," he says.

Take a breath, buddy! I'm just finding out about this and you already have me selling it off and more stipulations? What do I know about running a store or making anything work? I've never even held a real job. I'm too dumb for all this.

"Maybe I could use that glass of water. This is a lot to take in, and could I use your restroom?"

I need to think for a minute out of his gaze.

"Of course. My secretary will show you the way. It's just down the hall." He pushes a button on his phone. "Miss Fields, can you show Miss Penn the restroom and bring a glass of water?"

Intercoms sure are handy. Um, is there spinach in my teeth? This Fields chick is staring at me as she comes through the door. Does she smell horse doo-doo and think it's me?

"I'm so sorry for the loss of your friend," she says in a rush, leading me to the facilities. "I couldn't believe what happened to her, and when I read the will over and all to type up your papers, well, it's not really how things are done here on the island. No one would blame you if you sold it as soon as you could and headed back to your real life. Here's the bathroom."

Okay, she's nice, I'm just being a jerk. Cold water on my face might help. That should shock me into reality about this whole thing… it's feeling like a dream. I'm not doing very well with reality lately. Or ever. Take deep breaths. That's what mom always said when I was feeling this way. Compose yourself, think clearly. I wish I had someone better than myself to go to for pep talks. *Knute Rockne, All American*: "Win one for the Gipper." Maybe it doesn't apply, but it's the best I can do with all this stress. Where's Frapp when I need a good movie line? They probably think I got lost in here.

"Sorry, I needed a quick break and thanks for the water." I don't even remember bumbling my way back to Mr. Sawyer's office. "I have to ask, how did Theresa die?" I've wanted to know this since getting the bad news.

"I'm sorry, I thought you knew," Mr. Sawyer says.

"No, like I said, I haven't seen her in years, which is why I was very surprised to get the telegram. I wish I would have kept closer contact. You never think this could happen," I say.

"I'm sorry to say it was a sad ending. She was found sitting on a park bench early in the morning by one of the park custodians who thought she was sleeping. When he got near, it was apparent that she was dead, which of course was shocking for the fellow. The coroner's report confirmed a heart attack. She had been acting strangely and not keeping up with her store for the last several years. All her relatives were gone, and she kept to herself. It's quite tragic, really. Something must have happened along the way, but I don't know what."

"That is beyond sad. It was so long ago we spoke, and everything was fine then. Her aunt was still alive..."

"I guess you could say she became a recluse, and no one was close enough to her to do anything about it. When we saw the will, we thought maybe you could shed some light on her thinking, but that must not be the case either..." His voice trails off.

"Other than my summer here when I was in junior high, and several letters for a few years after that, we lost contact. I feel terrible, I had no idea."

"We may never know what was happening with her. She did have some clear thinking when it came to you, though. Besides the property, she has left a stipend to be used in the way she has directed. This stipend includes a three-month stay at the Grand Hotel here on the island with living and food expenses covered. It's an odd stipulation, but it is part of you getting the store and apartment above it. You must spend the three months on the island, and then you are free to sell. Again, the Sims-Dubois family is always interested in property. In fact, your new possession may be the only piece in the business district they don't already own. I, of course, have not shared any of this news with them so as not to break the confidentiality of the will, but it's no secret that even before Theresa owned the property, they were trying to get it from the previous owner who refused to sell it to them. So, I'm assuming it would be an easy sell for you at the end of three months."

And there it is. I guess I don't have to decide about selling and running the store right now. I have three months to figure out what to do next. Or, I'm trapped here on the island for three months, depending on how you look at it. I'll have to send Freddy a telegram and get him to sublease my apartment longer than I thought and ask him to keep it on the down-low, so I don't lose my subsidized housing. Living in San Fran is not cheap.

"Let me get this straight. The store and apartment aren't livable right now, so they need work. There's no inventory to bring in any income this tourist season. The earliest that could take place would be the next tourist season, after this winter," I say.

"Yes, and there is another designated stipend set aside to be used only for the restoration of the store and apartment," he adds.

"That means I have a place to live, a way to fix up the place—what about other money?"

I feel greedy asking, but this guy doesn't know my dire financial situation. This girl is broke.

"Unfortunately, that's all that's in the will. Living at the Grand Hotel, your food will all be included. I would suggest if you need more cash flow, you get a job for this tourist season on the island. There should be plenty of opportunities at the fudge shops, with the park system, or even at the Grand Hotel itself, although it would be odd to have someone living in the tourists' rooms working there," he concludes.

"Unbelievable. Seems like Trixie, that's what I called her, had plans for me in the back of her mind. She always was the one to plan our adventures and it looks like she's keeping her legacy alive."

"Yes, if you say so. If you agree, let's start signing papers. I'll have Miss Fields alert the Grand Hotel coach to pick up your luggage at the ferry office and then bring you up to your new home for the next few months. I don't know if you visited it while you were here last time, but it is quite opulent and fanciful. And the food—the best anywhere. You'll be living at one of the finest hotels in the world for a while. Quite a gift she left you. So, if you'll sign your full legal name starting here..."

"Don't say it, I'm not fond of my name, I go by my middle name, Piper. Please only call me Piper, or Miss Penn if you are more comfortable with that, but never my legal name. I mean you get it. You don't want people calling you Tom, right?"

"Tom? Uh, I thought I mentioned my name is William, but as you wish, Miss Penn. If you want to begin. There are quite a few papers to sign."

Tom Sawyer, I mentally shout. Geez, I would have to get another lawyer with zero sense of humor. Oh boy. Scribbling away, it's helping to pretend that I'm on a movie set signing autographs. The part of me with a foot in reality has a nagging feeling I should have another lawyer looking at all this, but who am I kidding? I don't have the money, the time, or the patience for more lawyers. I decided on the ferry ride over that Doris Day will give me the mantra for the day from *The Man Who Knew Too Much*—"Que Sera, Sera." It's quite poetic that as I'm signing the last paper, I hear a hauntingly familiar sound, the clip-clop of a horse close by. Funny, I can pick up on that sound, even inside this office.

"Your carriage awaits!" Miss Fields sure is peppy. Looking at them as they walk me out to the sidewalk, I want to grab them both and yell, "Help me! I don't know what I'm doing!" I know the look on my face probably conveys I am one cool chick; I would have made a great actress in Tinseltown. But, if they really knew me, they'd know the truth. I'm a basket case.

"Thank you, Mr. Sawyer. By the way, did you send some people to look for me in San Francisco?"

"Send people? No, we wouldn't do that," he says. "We would have made one more attempt to contact you. If we didn't hear something after a second telegram, we would have posted an additional notice in the paper. That's standard practice. No, we never send people. Why do you ask?"

"Yes, people from the firm are never sent, it's all done with telegrams and phone calls," Miss Fields adds.

"Not important, I've taken enough of your time. Thanks again," I say.

I guess the mystery of who talked to Frap will continue. Probably some scammers trying to steal from me, who thought I had something because of my dad. Boy, were they off the mark.

This is amazing, a beautiful glass-encased carriage complete with a driver wearing a top hat coming my way. Take that, BART and cable cars! Climbing the step up into the carriage, I can't believe I am about to become a resident of one of the swankiest hotels in America while concealing the fact I'm a broke lady with a criminal past. I feel like the Apple Annie character played by Bette Davis in *A Pocket Full of Miracles*. As she so aptly said as Margo Channing in *All About Eve*, "Fasten your seat belts. It's going to be a bumpy night." I haven't written to Bette Davis yet; she is due a letter.

Turning the corner and heading up the tree-lined road that leads to the Grand Hotel, I'm flooded with memories. There isn't anywhere like this in the world.

Chapter Six

The Annie Hall character said it best: "Well lah-de-dah, lah-de-dah."
So fancy.

There's no other word for the Grand Hotel. Looking at the long white porch with white wicker rocking chairs makes me catch my breath, even through the filmy pane of this carriage window.

The Straits of Mackinac gleaming in the sunshine like shimmering diamonds... I feel like a writer putting down words for a book. Regular thoughts, regular words, I can't find the right ones to encompass all that I'm feeling and seeing. So beautiful and pristine. "Gleaming in the sunlight" and "shimmering waves on sand", like I'm writing an 1800s novel. Memory after memory is coming back—Trixie and I sneaking in the back way through the tennis court, past the pool and the cascades of blooming lilacs, while running up the stairs to the porch before someone saw us—the thrill of pulling it off and being coconspirators—the delight of a true friend.

Seems like staying here for a three-month vacation, getting the store and apartment fixed up with the stipend, and selling it to start a new life away from subsidized housing in San Fran may all be one big reward for having a crappy life. Maybe that's how it works—pay your dues with problems, and then get a prize at the end. That's not the story I was told growing up, but then, I'm not sure about that story. Sitting on those stupid hard pews every time the doors were open at church gave me a lot of free time to think and imagine things. Sometimes I daydreamed about Jesus, so I didn't feel too bad about that. I wondered what it would have been like to be a sister in that family. If someone broke a clay pot, who got blamed? Obviously, Jesus didn't do it. She knew. He knew. It couldn't have been easy to have him for a brother.

My sister was the good twin, and I came off as the evil twin. The fact that she followed the rules turned me into even more of a rule-breaker. She didn't get the same grief from Dad when he went off on one of his tirades. Why would she? She never challenged him. Sometimes I hear his voice in my head, and I hate it. But he's gone and I'm here. Maybe I should pinch myself. Getting to live here for three months while my newly acquired business and apartment gets renovated seems, well, sinful.

I don't know what Trixie went through to provide this for me. I guess I'll never know. It's all too generous. She had no clue I would come to the island narrowly escaping jail time, with a pittance in my pocket. I shouldn't be broke. I should have had enough smarts to work a little instead of living off the small inheritance from my parents' life insurance. I also should have had enough brains not to steal, but maybe my dad was right. He told my sister and me whenever we goofed up, even when we were too young to understand—"When God was passing out brains, you thought he said 'trains', and you both said, 'I don't want one.'" The same guy who told the multitudes that God loves everyone showed us that he didn't mean his own family. But here I am. Me, someone who should be cast in a Ma and Pa Kettle movie, is going to live in the Grand Hotel. If God exists, He has an excellent sense of irony.

The reception desk lady says my room will be ready in an hour. I

31

don't mind. I'm just fine taking a rest in these wicker wonders that rock on this oh-so-very-long porch. What a view. The shiny Straits of Mackinac, and I can't stop looking at the Mackinac bridge and how it perfectly connects the upper and lower peninsula. That's it. No more thoughts about my Dad. I'm here on this porch and I'm going to relax. Most of the chairs are full but it doesn't feel crowded. I want to stop each tourist and tell them I get to live here, kind of rub it in, because most of them will be staying just a few days. That's a snotty thought. I sure hope this nice place will rub some nice off on me. This rocking back and forth is soothing and the sun feels so good on my face. Job number one—make time to sit on this porch every day. I need the calm. Close your eyes, Piper. Soak in the peace. Hope for a new start.

"Says here, longest porch in the world." With my eyes shut, I hear a voice in the next chair which I hoped would remain empty. Christopher Columbus! Now I have to see who is talking.

Ah, ha! It's an exuberant, very tanned young man reading the hotel pamphlet to a girl who looks at him like he's Christmas morning. Either they are dating or newly married, because she seems almost ready to jump up and kiss the guy. Close your eyes, Piper. Learn a thing or two more about this place. Why not be a fly on the wall for this little show that has presented itself. They remind me of Ali MacGraw and Ryan O'Neal in *Love Story*.

"You can only get to this island by ferryboat, and they don't allow any cars on the island. Just horses and bikes… ha! Look at this honey, five hundred horses on this island! See that pool down the hill? Esther Williams herself swam in that pool for the movie *This Time for Keeps*."

Don't do it, Piper. Keep your mouth shut, just listen and mind your own business.

"Yes, it's a 1947 movie also starring Jimmy Durante shot in part here at the Grand Hotel and I recommend it if you ever get a chance to see it," I say.

I can't resist spouting movie info. It's like a curse or something, I can't shut up.

"You don't say... hear that, Marilyn? We should see if we can ever see that movie! Are you here for the first time too? I'm Tanner and this is my wife, Marilyn," he says.

"We're on our honeymoon," Marilyn says.

I hit the nail on the head. People don't look at each other this way after a while. They're newlyweds, all right. And, funny, I just wrote to Marilyn, and now I meet a Marilyn.

"It's going to be my first time staying at the Grand Hotel. I walked through once many years ago when I was a kid. But it sure is something," I say.

They are adorable.

"We're from Florida, but a buddy of mine works here at the hotel, so he got us a nice discount for this trip. Oh wait, I don't think I'm supposed to let that part out," Tanner says.

"It's okay, I can keep a secret," I say.

"Speak of the devil—here he is now... Cam the man!" Tanner says, greeting his friend.

"Tanner and Marilyn, you made it! Welcome to our little piece of paradise! Glad it worked out for you to spend a few days here." Their friend sure has a nice smile.

"Oh, I'm sorry, that's rude of me, did you bring a friend?" he asks.

"No, just met her here on the porch, and I didn't get your name Miss..." Tanner says.

"Piper Penn. I'm a guest here for a while."

Why am I giving out my real name? I thought I was going to come up with some charade while here to keep my business in town to myself. Too late now. A townie has my real name. I guess in a place this small trying to be two people wouldn't work anyway.

"Hi, Piper, I'm Cam. I work on the grounds so you may see me around a bit."

Um, Mr. Red Head, that would not be a hardship, unless you're married or attached.

"Well, let's get some lunch, guys. I've got a reservation in the dining hall for us. I'm sorry, Piper, would you like to come?" Cam asks.

Polite too. Kind of a Danny Kaye vibe from *White Christmas*. I suddenly realize that three people are staring at me while I'm off in Pine Tree, Vermont, getting ready to do a sister act.

"Oh, you go on, my room will be ready any minute, and I really want to get settled. Thanks, though. I'm sure I'll see you around the hotel," I say.

"She knows a lot about this hotel, even told us about a movie that was filmed here with Esther Williams and Jimmy Durante," Marilyn says.

"Yah, that's part of the Hollywood history here, but here's an inside scoop. They're going to be filming another movie here soon. A bunch of us might try out for the extras. They're looking for island people to fill in some of the slots not taken by the professional actors," Cam says.

A movie? Here? This stay just got better. Gosh, I wish I was better at showing my poker face. But, inside I'm jumping up and down. Pick me! Pick me!

"I'm here for a few months, I might be interested in finding out more about that," I say. I hope I came off with my act together. I'm trying not to show my idiot side right away, especially in front of this adorable redhead.

"Ask the concierge on duty, she will have the information. It's a period piece I think, set back in history. Could be a cool thing to do. See yah around, Piper," Cam says.

"Nice to meet you, Piper," Tanner and Marilyn say at the same time. Then they do that adoring look into each other's eyes. Kind of like

Cary Grant looks at Deborah Kerr in *An Affair to Remember*. Marriages always start out so nice.

"Nice to meet you all, and toodle-ooh."

I just said a phrase I have never said before in my life. I don't know why I picked this exact moment in history to say it, especially when I could have done something to impress Mr. Red. People from San Fran don't say 'toodle-ooh'. Must be jet lag.

Ah good, it's one, and my room should be ready. I hope I like what they've picked to be my home-sweet-home for the next few months. My key says third floor, which should give a nice view.

These stairs aren't too bad, good exercise. The spy in me likes peeking in every room with a door open as a maid cleans. Walls with flowers, cats, plaids, dogs, nautical themes, Chinese symbols blend with carpeting full of swirls, zigs and zags, and arrows. This is not what I'm used to in decorating, all thrown together like an interior designer on a bad trip. Funny thing—it all works. It looks classy and creative. Their decorator is not timid.

"Thanks for bringing my bags," I say to the porter, "and here's a dollar for your trouble. I'm sorry, it isn't more." I'm not prepared for high-society and tipping people.

"Oh, miss, there is no tipping at the Grand Hotel. It was my pleasure to serve you," he says.

Yes! Miss! See, no "ma'am" here. I love this place. All right Room 308, I like it. Eight is my favorite number. Wow! A very fluffy canopy bed—soft, billowy, and perfect.

Check.

I have a balcony! The view of Round Island Lighthouse is like looking at a postcard and the little reading chair and desk in the corner will be ideal for gazing out the glass doors while I do watercolors. This is all coming together nicely. A big step up from the slum style I'm used to with tag-sale furniture.

Check.

A canopy bed! I have never slept in a canopy bed. Wait, I did once, now that I think of it. We were on the missionary traveling dog and pony show and we always stayed at the homes of church people. My sister and I slept in a canopy bed and I remember waking up and thinking I was seeing clouds. Man, my memory sensors are on overload. This island has magic or something. Nice closet space. I don't have a lot but good spots for art supplies. And I'm digging this ambiance—a nautical theme with lighthouses—even in the bathroom. These are the softest, biggest, most luxurious towels, like velvety fields of cotton. Until this exact moment I didn't realize how I've lived with scratchy towels my whole life.

Check.

Be still my heart. A girl could get used to this if a girl had a few kazillion dollars. But a girl could also feel super-guilty about how she got this room for three months. A girl could also pass out if she doesn't get something to eat soon. Free pass in the dining hall, here I come.

Opulent. That's the word I've been trying to find in my memory somewhere. This is beyond fancy, it's opulent, king and queen kind of territory. Yes, thank you, I will sit here. The most elegantly clad gentleman escorts me to a window seat. I've already learned from some parlor eavesdropping that most people working here are from Jamaica.

Let's see. White fish done to perfection. Crusty hard rolls, a salad with beautiful ripe vegetables and lettuce with all kinds of colors I'm not used to. The most tender baby red potatoes with butter and parsley I've ever had. It all works together in this chandeliered, gleaming, Cinderella-like dining room, and it's taking care of my shaking feeling. That helps with my brain acting goofy too. This is how it feels to live like royalty. After dining on Ramen noodles and day-old donuts for some time now, I find this mind-boggling.

Ah, the dessert bar. Let's see. There is more than fudge on this island. A small strawberry tart and a tiny piece of luscious chocolate cake with chocolate frosting and… stop. A girl must keep her figure with redheads roaming around. I do love Lucy, and she's my favorite redhead, but guys with red hair also trip my trigger. Outside of Danny Kaye they seem to be a rarity. Red Skelton, Red Buttons… yah, it's hard to think of redheads.

"Miss, there's a message for you."

The waiter wakes me out of my redheaded Hollywood daydream. This is a much better way to get a message, on a small silver tray. Wait, a message? Who even knows I'm here? And what's with people giving me messages?

Welcome to the island, Miss Penn! As the chairwoman of the Mackinac Island Town Board and one of the original family members of beautiful Mackinac Island, I would love to have high tea with you at the Grand Hotel today. I will be waiting for you in the lobby at three sharp on the large floral couch in the center of the room.

Kind regards,

Katherine Sims-Dubois

High tea with this big-shot lady? Even though my lawyer can't talk about me, evidently gossip is not off-limits to anyone else on the island. High tea—wow! Did I just step into some alternate universe where I make good decisions, and all is right with the world? I think I'm far more comfortable in a world where good guys finish last and people get what they have coming.

I was brought up to believe that if you just asked for forgiveness for your sins, voila! You could become whiter than snow. But I don't know if I follow. From what I've seen, you often get what you have coming, except for the innocents you bring along with you. It all makes my head hurt. I don't know what I believe. But I know I better quit going off on these thought tangents and get ready for meeting this island belle of the ball. She sounds like a doozy. Thank goodness there's time for a quick stop in my new nest. Yes, a redo on my lip gloss is in order. Forget the gloss, look at this room! I'm staying in the Grand Hotel, getting ready for high tea with Katherine Sims-Dubois. That's a whole bunch of words strung together that I'm not used to having in my brain. Since they have this high tea hootenanny every afternoon in the Grand main lobby, I guess she thinks it's a good place to meet. I'm not sure exactly why we're meeting, but it's better if I stop overthinking things. Be on time. Make a good impression. It's the new me. Now, I'm an on-time, high-tea-drinking, high-living girl in a new town with a new future, waiting for the other shoe to drop. Optimistic, but not stupid. I didn't just fall off the turnip truck yesterday, as Freddy says—something must give. It will drop, with a big loud "thud," no doubt, but in the meantime, I'm going to "while away an hour", as my favorite scarecrow would say.

I must pay attention to time now because this place has lots of rules about when things happen and what you can and can't wear. I'm here, in the Grand Hotel, and it's not costing me a dime. I must be dreaming, but this is better than any dream I've had lately. The water, the sheer beauty of being in a place that pays attention to every detail. A girl could get used to this. But now it's time to head to the parlor, or close enough. Nothing wrong with doing more room-peeking on the trip down. I haven't seen a duplicate yet. Each one is different. Who is this designer? The variety blows me away. There's the large floral couch, and there she is. I thought I was early.

"You must be Piper Penn. I'm Katherine Sims-Dubois, town chair-woman and unofficial welcome committee for the island. Please, have a seat and a cup of tea!"

With her high beehive hairdo and long red nails perfectly matching the red cherries on her fluffy white dress with the small black shawl, she is a vision. I can truthfully say I have never seen anyone like this outside of a movie screen or a cartoon. There are even small cherries on her black pumps. Where do you even buy shoes like this? Oh my gosh, listening to her say some niceties to me, I'm picking up an accent I've heard in the old '30s and '40s movies. The Transatlantic accent I think they call it. That boarding school, quasi-English feel, with softer vowels and quick, sharp *t*'s—yeah, she's got it down. The nasal, clipped pronunciation almost makes me want to burst out laughing. Doesn't she know that no one really talks like this, well not at least since World War II was over? But, this lah-de-dah flavor does seem to suit this wild character that is Katherine Sims-Dubois! Bette Davis and Katharine Hepburn should be here with us' they had the diction down, perfectly. I'll have to pay close attention if she drops her *r*'s in words like '*winnah*' or '*timbah*' for 'winner' and 'timber'. 'Dance' might become '*donse*'. I wish I had a movie camera.

"Oh, I thought I was early, but I hope I haven't kept you waiting, Mrs. Dubois."

"Please, call me Katherine. We aren't very formal around here, I'm sure."

Yes, it's all there and the fast speed too! Ironic that we're at high tea with finger sandwiches and teacups that probably cost more than I make in a year. Not formal? You've got to be kidding.

"Thank you, Katherine, I wasn't sure how you even knew I was here."

"Oh, Piper, you'll learn soon enough that very little gets by me on my island. I feel so bonded to this place because my heritage goes far back into the history of this land. Well, not as far back as the Native Americans of course, but right after! Our bloodlines go back to the *Mayflower*, and when I married Mr. Dubois, uniting the two main families of the island, the Simses and the Duboises, we brought together a beautiful blood lineage of all those who came before us that continues to this day. Guardians of the island! Other than my short stint in a British boarding school, I have only ever been on this fantastic island, you see. This island and I are soul mates. I'm sure that's evident to all."

Oh my gosh, this lady is ready for her close-up, Mr. DeMille. And that solves the mystery of where she picked up the accent—British boarding school it is. Is she really doing all this grand gesturing just for me or because the rest of the room is looking?

"Now with my dear Mr. Dubois gone on beyond, it has turned to me to be the matriarch of our lineage and well-being," she says.

"I understand that you also own most of the property and stores on Main and Market Streets?" I ask.

"Why, yes, seems news gets around fast to the newcomers too. Now, I don't want you to think that's the only reason I wanted to meet you. Although, I do believe I could be of great service to you in being able to get back to your life in... where are you from?"

"San Francisco."

"Oh, San Francisco. It must have been hard for you to leave your cozy life there, I'm sure, to come to a new place, all alone. Let's face it, there's not a thriving night life for young people here on the island," she says. "Our island is not like the British Isles that teem with dance and culture."

She said it, "donse", and the soft *t* on 'culture'.

"I'm taking it one day at a time. I will be here for a few months to get my bearings and then, we'll see. I'm going to get to know the place, and then I'll know what my options are," I say.

"Have you had a chance to meet anyone yet?" Katherine asks.

"Not really, I just arrived today. I'm sure I'll meet people as time goes on."

It's taking every ounce of my self-control not to imitate her accent. I feel like I've walked into an old movie set.

"Well, the concierge here is a good friend, so she will be helpful to answer any questions. Another cousin's son works on the grounds, but he's not very fond of me. Actually, he's not a blood relative... adopted as a child, he and his siblings. That accounts for the flaming red hair that you can't miss. His sister had a baby out of wedlock, and I think he's got a brother who is in jail downstate—some sort of troublemaker into all manner of ill things. They weren't raised on the island like most of the relatives, but there are black sheep in every family, aren't there? Their parents bolted as soon as they were out of high school and got married right away. Truth be told, they just don't fit here. Even when they would come back for visits, they never even stopped to see me, just some of the other no-account cousins. I was surprised he's back on the island. I offered him a job with the family businesses, but he was rather rude to me. Guess that's a trait of redheads, along with a temper. I'm sure you'll run into him here at the Grand. Tell him cousin Katherine says hello!" she says, half-singing.

She must be talking about Cam. I don't know how I feel about the fact that she spilled his story when I was aching to hear it from him. He's all jeans and T-shirt, and she's, well, in a class by herself. I bet some alternative form of *Vogue* is her fashion bible. So, Mr. Cam, there's a bit of mystery here between you and the lady with cherries on her shoes.

"Well, I have gone on and it's time for me to run, but remember, Piper, we are a very generous people. I'm sure you'll need to do some improvements on Theresa's old place. You will be needing building permits and such from the town board. And of course, if you are interested in selling, you will be treated very fairly. Please do let me know if there's anything I can do to make your stay here enjoyable. As I mentioned, I know everyone, and pretty much everything. It's my life passion! And I'm very sorry about your friend. Had we understood what was happening with her, we would have stepped in to help. I've taken it upon myself to raise some funds to start a scholarship for the island school in her name," Katherine says.

"Well, that would be a nice tribute," I say.

Maybe she is over the top, but that is a very nice gesture.

"Yes, it's how we take care of one another here for the people who fit. You'll see. Well, I've kept you long enough, and do keep in touch, but I know where to find you!" she says, this time fully singing the words.

With a quick kiss on my cheek and a swish of her skirt filled with cherries, Katherine Sims-Dubois is gone, waving at various people while she makes an exaggerated exit to the porch.

Interesting. Mr. Red—Cam the Man—is not in good graces with his powerful relative. I'm sure he'll have the lowdown on Katherine's story. I can't wait to find out more. Now that this obligation is over, I want to hit up her concierge friend and get the scoop on that movie Cam mentioned. Talk about timing, this is incredible. I think her desk is at the far end of the parlor, past the row of couches and the big piano...

"Oh, careful there." Oops. Well, hello tall, dark, and handsome. His voice is deep and soothing.

"Oh my gosh, I'm so sorry!" Apparently, I just backed into this amazing specimen of a man and I stepped on his toes!

"I didn't... I wasn't..." I've lost the ability to speak. Gosh, he's good-looking. Such a noble face, dark hair, and he looks like a movie star.

"It's okay, things happen. I get lost in daydreams too," he says.

"So sorry, sir, I hope I didn't hurt you."

"I'm fine, don't give it a second thought. Enjoy your day."

My face must be twenty shades of red. I just want to stop at the concierge desk and head back to my room. Man, is he handsome and I feel like I know him already. How embarrassing, I'm such a klutz! That's it, concierge stop and then I'm bolting.

"Hello! I've been waiting for you!" The concierge seems very happy to see me.

"Thanks, I was wondering about the movie coming..." Before I can finish, she gives me a shove and I barely catch myself from hitting the ground. She's not talking to me! She's heading toward Mr. Handsome who has a crowd gathering around him.

"Christopher! Mr. Reeve! Here, come with me, the director is waiting in a private dining area," the concierge says.

So, I just bumped into Christopher Reeve, almost broke his foot, and I didn't even recognize him. I injured Superman. Now we're back on track. This seems more normal. He must be here for the new movie. My stay just got a lot more interesting. Maybe Christopher will have an alternate love interest, and I could get the part! Maybe I can get to know Superman on a personal level. Maybe Mr. Red and Superman will fight over me.

Maybe, I'm losing my mind.

Chapter Seven

The movie is going to be called *Somewhere in Time* starring Christopher Reeve, Jane Seymour, and Christopher Plummer. It involves time travel, and it's mostly being shot right here on the island in the next few months. Later, when the concierge had landed back on earth, I got the scoop and the application to apply to be an extra. The best part of the audition process was waiting in line next to Cam, who was also trying out for a part.

"Hey, you decided to try out huh?" Cam asks.

"Yes, I love movies, so the chance to see one up close is too good to pass up. You have the acting bug as well?" I ask.

"I'm trying out, but I'm going to make it clear that I only want a part that doesn't take up too much time," Cam says. "My first priority is my job. Our hotel owner encouraged us to be a part of the process. He's a great boss. Are you enjoying your stay so far?"

"It's amazing. I'm here for a few months, but believe me, this is life far above my pay grade. Hey, I met your cousin the other day. She said to say hello."

"Oh, you met the Queen of the Island, huh? That's too bad."

"I'm sensing there's no love lost on either side. She knows you aren't fond of her."

"She is something else, I guess that's a polite way to put it. Yah, I keep my distance from that one. My parents had nothing nice to say about the way she treated them when they were kids growing up here. In fact, she's a big reason they didn't stay on the island and moved downstate to start their life. We would come back for some short vacations, but even then, she harassed them and was just mean. I have never quite understood what her problem is, but she's nasty. I really don't know many people that I would ever say that about, but she is someone I never need to see again. I fell in love with the place despite her, and always knew I would try to get back here somehow—but not on her dime."

Okay, Piper. Don't let this chance pass you by.

"Looks like you're up next. wanna catch a cup of coffee after these auditions?" I ask.

I'm getting very brave in my old age, but how else am I going to meet people on this isolated little lot of land? Tourists are here for a few days and gone, so I need to make some friends with the locals. And, I admit it. He's cute. No one is really allowed near Superman, so I'll go with Mr. Red.

"Sure, wanna meet in the café downstairs at three?"

"Sounds perfect. I'll see you then."

As if on cue, the casting director calls out his name: Cam Nelson.

"Break a leg," I say. So showbizzy. I always wanted to say that.

I hand in my short form when my name is called, and I'm hoping to wow them with my little audition piece I memorized.

"So, you're from California, huh? That's where most of us are from. You're out of your element here! Will you be here for a few months? That's how long we anticipate shooting the scenes here on the island," the assistant director says.

"Yes, three months at least. In fact, I live right here in the hotel," I say.

"No real acting experience, but you're not shy in front of the camera, are you?" he asks.

"Um, I don't think so. I think I take direction pretty well," I say.

"It's important to keep your focus on what you're doing and don't look awkwardly at the actors. You need to blend into the background. Do you think you can do that?" he asks.

"I'm a blender from way back." Oh my gosh, I come up with the dumbest things to say at the worst moments.

In this grand, less-than-two-minute audition I'm asked to look left and look right. Then I'm handed a card with my part—Maid-Role: Scrubs the floor and dusts. I'd like to thank the Academy. The card has my next few call times and a stern warning not to interact with the stars. Oh my, the glamour. Talking to Katherine was more dramatic than the role I got. Whatever. It's something. I've got some time to do some watercolors before I meet Cam for coffee.

Leaving my watercolor paper and paints all set up on my desk facing the deck so I can paint every spare moment is turning out to be a good idea. I am constantly inspired to paint. Sticking to postcard-size paintings allows me to get a lot done, and I think that's what tourists will want to take home. Selling them to make extra dough is part of my grand scheme to survive. Heading back to my room, I see the splashes of the various blues in the water lapping up against the small speck of land that houses Round Island lighthouse. The view from my balcony and window are perfect for an artist. I don't know if I get to call myself an artist, I just paint. I want to paint the bridge too, and the Straits of Mackinac that run underneath connecting Lake Michigan to Lake Huron. To think that people used to have to wait in long lines to take the ferry across with their cars with the bridge not there until 1957.

I amaze myself on how I'm becoming a student of this place. I like to stop and read the walls of the lower lobby. They're filled with newspaper and magazine clippings, framed to tell the history of this glorious building. Each step is like a fantastic history lesson. I imagine what it must have been like, getting from Lower Michigan to Upper Michigan when people used to wait with their '57 Chevy cars to board the ferry and cross the water. It was a day-long event, especially during busy times like hunting season. Five men even died during the construction of the bridge. What about before that, what the Indians and the missionaries went through in their birch-bark canoes? I have no idea if the natives took kindly to the Jesuit priests who showed up, probably because Walter Cronkite wasn't around to tell the story. We may never know. Sooner than I expect, it's time to meet Cam for coffee.

* * *

"Ahh, it feels good to take a moment to sit down and take a break. I hope I didn't keep you waiting long!" Cam says as he sits down.

"You've been busy since I saw you at the audition, huh?" I ask.

"Always, work is very busy. I must be crazy to audition, but I made it clear that my job comes first, so they agreed to use me as a fill-in in some scenes, probably a waiter or butler type."

"I was equally blessed with a major part—maid scrubbing floor."

"Oh, come on, you should get a bigger part! I don't know that much about the movie, but I bet you would be great."

"I'm really happy just to get to see how a movie is made. I am pretty crazy about movies in general so this will be a thrill, and I didn't even know this was happening, so it's all cool. I don't know how much I could handle. It's been a bit of a whirlwind to get here and get settled."

"What can I get you fine folks this day?" our waiter asks.

"Coffee sounds good to me. Piper, what would you like?"

"Coffee with cream is perfect, thanks," I say.

"I'll make sure it's fresh and hot, my lady. Coming right up." Our waiter leaves to get the coffee.

"I love how the gentlemen talk here. Chivalry is not dead!" I say.

"The people working here for the most part are really nice. They care about the guests, and I'm glad that shows," Cam says. "They work here for 'the season', as it's called, and then go back to Jamaica to work there, because the two tourist seasons dovetail perfectly. Many of them are here to support their families. They can make so much more here than in their own country."

"All the porters and waiters seem to be from Jamaica. Don't local people want to work here too? Is it some kind of rule who can work here?" I ask.

"I think they would love to hire people from the mainland, or from Michigan in general, but they simply aren't coming here to work the short season." Cam explains. "Most of the hospitality industry is open year-round. We close late fall. It's not that easy to get here either. The Grand has very high standards for levels of service which is shared by the tourism industry in Jamaica. My situation is a little different, there's maintenance to do year-round, so I can live here all year."

"You really love this place and what it stands for, I can tell," I say.

"Thanks, that's quite a compliment, because I do feel that way. This place is real… an authentic, genuine place to be, and that's what draws me and gets me through even hard days. I've had a lot of the opposite experiences in life, and I just don't have the stomach for it anymore. I'm into real things."

"I hear ya. Hypocrisy has messed me up in life, and as you say, I just don't have the stomach for it, but let me be truthful. I've been the hypocrite myself, way more times than I'd like to admit to someone like you. Maybe this fresh air and pristine atmosphere will put me on the right path," I say.

"Here are your coffees, Mr. Cam and milady, and cream. And a plate of cookies and fudge as our compliment. Enjoy."

Our waiter pours the fresh hot joe.

"Oh nice! We must have coffee more often. I don't always get this kind of sweet treat, complimentary style! Here, help yourself," Cam says.

"Just one small piece of fudge for me. I think you could put on a lot of pounds around this place if you don't watch it. You're out doing all that physical labor, while I'm sitting in my room painting, so you go crazy and enjoy!" I say.

"Painting, huh? What medium? My mom loved to paint, and she did different types," Cam says.

"Watercolor mostly. Sometimes I dabble in acrylics, like a mixed medium with ink too, depending on what I think will work. I'm a self-taught painter, so I guess I don't know the rules. I just do what seems right to me. Since I got here, with all this amazing scenery, I just want to paint, and paint, and paint. But watercolors are my favorite, because you never know what the water will do. It has a mind of its own and can change the painting. I love that," I say.

"Very cool, I hope I get to see some of these paintings sometime, especially how you see the island as someone so new. That would be interesting."

"I hope I didn't oversell myself, I mean, I'm no Picasso!"

"I bet you're great, and I hope I didn't come off as Saint Cam or something before, because I'm not. But I do believe in change, and changing for the better, and that it's possible. But I'm getting in way too deep here. So, milady, Miss Piper, what the heck are you doing here at the Grand Hotel? You said it's not your norm, so there's more to your story."

"Oh, don't I come off as a very rich girl, just whiling away the summer? Because that's not the case, let me assure you. I'm from San Francisco, and I was here in junior high for a summer with a childhood friend, who I called Trixie. The island knows her as Theresa Post, and you probably heard of her passing."

"I'm so sorry. Yes, it was so sad. That kind of news gets around fast in a place this size. I knew her a little, just to say 'hello' when walking by. The last year or so, I heard gossip about something being wrong with her, that she wasn't acting normal. It seemed that no one was close enough to her to do something about it. Or, maybe that's our way of making ourselves feel better about the fact that no one took ownership for helping the poor girl. I guess everyone thought someone else would do it. That's sad to say now, but I do think that's what happened. Everyone feels bad that we didn't see it as a community. I think we learned a lesson about reaching out to people."

"I feel horrible, because we had lost touch in the last few years, and I had no idea at all. And then I find out she left me her store and apartment in her will, which just adds to my bad feelings."

"She left you her store and place on Market Street?" Cam asks. "Well, you had to be a little freaked out to get the news and leave San Francisco to head to this tiny part of the world. How are you handling all of this? Is your family going to come and help you get settled?"

"No, no, I'm on my own with this."

I don't know this guy well enough to lay the story of my family on him.

"Your cousin Katherine offered to buy the place. But confidentially, I have to fulfill a will stipulation that I stay here for three months. She doesn't know that, and I think I'll keep it to myself, if you wouldn't mind not telling anyone."

What's with me? I don't tell him about my family, but I tell him something important about the will. Hopefully, he can't stand her as much as he says, and will not say anything. He seems trustworthy.

"Scout's honor, I won't say anything. I'm sure she would love to buy the place. I think that's the last piece of property that the Sims-Dubois families don't own, and she wants it bad. She's always wanted to own all of the island that isn't designated as a state park, and that one small piece of property prevents her from that goal."

"Not to change the subject, but do you like watching movies, Cam?" I ask.

"Yah, I don't have much time, but I enjoy a good movie, for sure. Why do you ask?" Cam says with a smile. Oh, that's a nice smile.

"Because I'm feeling like someone from one of my favorite movies, *The Wizard of Oz*. Dorothy has the shoes the witch wants, and that makes you Glinda, telling me not to take off the shoes," I say.

"Ha! No, Piper of Oz, you do whatever you think is best with the property. I have no opinion either way other than I like the idea of the Queen not getting what she wants, but that's not a good attitude, and I'm working on having one of those. But you met her. You see what I mean, don't you?" Cam asks.

"Oh yes, I see it. She comes off as *c-r-a-z-y*, and that accent! Not like anyone around here. She's stuck in a 1930s movie," I say.

"My Mom actually picked up on that. Katharine didn't grow up talking like that. She went to a boarding school in England for a summer and came back talking that way. I don't think she knows that everyone on the island makes fun of the way she talks behind her back, but they are also afraid of her because she wields so much power if you work for her, and just about everyone does."

"She's just being super-nice to me at the moment, because she wants me to sell it to her. She did tell me she knows everyone and everything that happens on the island, which is a scary statement."

"It's telephone, telegraph, and tell-a-Katherine, as far as the gossip train goes here on the island," Cam replies. "She makes it her business to be the town busybody, if you ask me. I think our concierge is her line to hotel news. They were childhood friends. I make sure to stay out of her way when I can just because of that. Anyway, enough about strange relations. Do you think you want to get the place back into shape and sell things next tourist season? I mean the new season is starting now, so you're out of luck for this year. I would imagine you buy gift merchandise over the winter to be ready for the tourist season next spring. I'm only asking because some guys who work with me here at the Grand are good carpenters and would probably take on some side work. They won't charge you an arm and a leg. They aren't the kind who would give any extra time to a movie, but they love side carpentry work. I will vouch for their character as good honest workers."

So, are you looking out for my well-being Mr. Red? I haven't had anyone do that in a long time, I kind of like it. You are becoming more and more interesting to me.

"That's good because I have a budget I must stick with," I say. "I don't have much cash flow of my own. I'm not from money, but Trixie did leave a stipend designated for remodeling. It's amazing how detailed the will is, considering she passed so young, almost as if she knew she wouldn't be here for long. But why she chose me, I still don't know. We were very close that one summer, but not much after that.".

"Well, she must have had very fond thoughts of you and your time here, and with her great aunt gone for a few years, she really wasn't close to anyone here, I don't think. It's a good lesson for me to pay attention to people more. I get very involved in my work on the grounds, and I can ignore everything going on around me. I've always been that way, kind of keeping to myself. Oh my gosh, listen to me, I sound like I'm on Phil Donahue. I don't even know you very well, and I'm getting all deep or whatever. I'm sorry."

"It's okay, Cam, maybe it's a growing-up thing. I've regretted some things recently because I was so focused on myself, I missed what was happening. I've been stuck on thinking about myself nonstop the last few years, and frankly, I'm tired of me." My admission surprises even me. "Wow, what's in that coffee, some kind of truth serum?"

"I know. As long as we're telling truthful things, let me guess your age. Twenty-two or twenty-three?" Cam asks.

"Very good. Twenty-three, almost twenty-four. How did you know?" I ask, leaning in and giving him a wink.

"I might have guessed older because you seem mature, but then telling a lady she's older, I'm no dummy!"

"Okay, Mr. Smartie, my turn. You are either twenty-seven or twenty-nine. One of those."

"Neither. I'm twenty-eight, and not turning twenty-nine until next year. So, I win the age contest. I will reward myself with another cookie, and then, Miss Penn, I do need to get back to my planting. Hey, this has been fun. I hope we can do coffee again soon."

"I would love that. I'm on my own here, and you sir are my first real friend, unless you count the queen of the island!"

Cam groans. I see how to stay on your good side, Mr. Handsome. Don't talk about your pushy relative.

"Just kidding," I reassure him. "I love movies, but real-life drama queens are a bit much to handle. I would like it if you could help me with contacting the carpenter guys you know. I guess getting an estimate would be the first step."

"Sure, it's Ben and Joel Conrad—they're brothers. I'll come along if you'd like and help get things going. Between all of us, we can get some good ideas about what do to with everything. I'll contact the guys and see what will work."

"Thanks, Cam, that would be a big help. It's all a little overwhelming."

"Hang in there, Piper. You're staying at the Grand on Mackinac Island, life is good."

"Seems a lot of people here have that same idea."

I'm not sure if it's life on the island, or finally getting to have a friend. I've spent so much time in my own head, it's fun to talk to someone. I really want to get to know him better. He's going to be a good sounding-board with all these decisions I'll have to make.

Heading back to my room, the nagging state of my pathetic finances is starting to weigh on me. Even though so many things are paid for, I still need money to live. Plus, there's my apartment in San Francisco hanging over my head. The movie part is a pittance, but it's something, more about bragging rights than anything else. Freddy promised to try to sublet for me, but he must be careful who he works with because it's against the rules to sublet subsidized housing.

Two ideas are muddling around in my head. I'm going to check out the Catholic Church bingo sign I saw hanging up in the drugstore in town to see if they need a bingo caller, something I actually have experience with in San Francisco. And, I'm going to see if the Grand Hotel gift shop will take some of my watercolor paintings of the hotel and put them up for sale. Maybe between the two I can get by. First stop—bingo.

Chapter Eight

"I'm sorry, I was looking for the priest, is he here by chance?"

I can't believe I'm calling out to a nun from the back of the church.

"No, he only comes for Sunday mass, from the mainland. He's not here during the week. I'm the one who holds down the fort here at St. Anne's." She is a very tiny nun, which is more evident the closer she gets.

I've never really talked in person to a nun before, but I have secretly admired them since I was a kid. From *The Flying Nun*, to Hayley Mills in *The Trouble with Angels*, to *Sound of Music* and seeing Mary Tyler Moore as a nun being pursued by Elvis, I've daydreamed about being that kind of sister. I just hadn't seen any instances of Protestant girls achieving nun status.

"Was there something I could help you with? I try to be the eyes and ears of the church during the week when Father Michaels is not available," she says.

"I don't know, I just thought maybe I would talk with him about some things, but I'm not Catholic, so maybe I don't qualify, or whatever." I'm doing my stupid talk again, and I seem to be getting better at it, especially when I'm nervous.

"I don't think being Catholic is a qualification for having a talk, but I wonder if I might be an ear for you? I'm Sister Mary-Margaret, by the way, and you are?"

"Oh, sorry, that's rude of me. I'm Piper Penn. Sister, Mary, Ma'am, Your Nunness."

I am a certified idiot. 'Your Nunness'?

"Nice to meet you, Piper. Are you here for a visit on the island?"

She's probably busy, I better get to why I'm here.

"Actually, I'm here for a few months. I inherited a little store from Trixie, or Theresa as you may have known her—the one on Market Street," I say.

"Oh, yes, that was a tragedy. I heard about it from one of the parishioners who knew about it. So, you're her relation?" Sister asks.

"No, actually, we were childhood friends, and I was pretty surprised to get the telegram at my place in San Francisco. I was shocked to hear she had passed and to find out she had left her place to me."

"That sounds like an amazing turn of events. Listen, I was just about to lock up here and head downstairs to my living quarters, sit down with some popcorn and a cola, and enjoy my weekly date with my favorite show—*I Love Lucy*, you know the old black and white ones. I'd love some company. Why don't you join me?"

Nuns watch *I Love Lucy* in their spare time? I think she's about ten years older than me, so she probably didn't see it in the first run either.

"You watch *I Love Lucy*? It was my mom's favorite show, so I was always along for the ride and eventually became a fan too. I watched it with my old neighbor in San Francisco, but, hey, I don't want to mess up your free time," I say.

"I'd love the company," she repeats. "Follow me, watch your step on these stairs, they're a little steep. This is the rectory—our convent, really—where I live with Sister Albertina. She's gone back to the Philippines for a few months because her mother is ill. This used to be where the priest lived but having us nuns here to assist Father Michaels is what has worked out best here on the island."

So, this is where island kids snuck in to steal some sacramental wine and smoke cigars? It's probably not a good idea to always base your opinion of real people on movie and TV shows you've seen. Located right next to the furnace room, it's clear that anyone who lives here has tried to lose the basement feel with cheery posters along the wall. It obviously was not originally meant to be a home for anyone, but I can sense this nun turns wherever she is into something fun and homey.

"My mom even dyed her hair red once, but it didn't go over well on the home front, so she went back to being a blonde. My sister and I loved it. She would take us along to see *I Love Lucy* anywhere she could, even before cable made it available. In San Francisco, there's all kinds of weird little theaters to catch things. There was even a church that showed episodes weekly after bingo. So here we were, a pastor's family sneaking off on a church night, when my dad was out of town, to see Lucy!"

I sure do babble a lot since I arrived on this island.

"I love that! Kind of Lucy life lessons, I totally get that. Did your family come with you to claim your inheritance?" she asks, gesturing me to take a seat on an old flowered couch.

Sitting down, I feel some tears. Maybe it's the mustiness of the basement causing allergies or something. I cry at the most inconvenient times, but when I'm supposed to, nothing. Why am I crying now? This must be some kind of nun juju.

"I'm so sorry, Piper, did I say something wrong?" Sister asks as she sits down next to me.

"No, I'm sorry, you are being so nice. I don't usually cry. It's been over four years. My family was all killed, murdered really, in Africa. It's just me. Honestly, I don't usually start crying every time I talk about it. Maybe because it's the church or something, and maybe because you're a nun... I've got a nun-thing... I don't know, I'm blabbering."

"Nun thing? Don't tell me you were treated unkindly by a nun or something like that. I hope I don't frighten you in any way!"

"No, quite the opposite. My Dad was a Protestant evangelist and eventually was on TV. You can imagine I have not met many nuns in real life, but I've always loved nuns... well at least on TV and in the movies. I know that's kind of dumb, and when I hear myself say it out loud, it sounds really stupid. But Hayley Mills... Julie Andrews... Sally Fields... *Lilies of the Field, The Sound of Music, The Flying Nun,* everything I saw made me want to be a nun. Honestly, I've never voiced this out loud and never to another person and never to a nun! You must think I'm loony tunes. But I'm not lying, I just loved nuns in shows. The more I talk the sillier I'm sounding—forgive me."

"Don't apologize. In fact, truth be told, it's probably some of the reasons I started looking into becoming a nun myself—Hayley Mills smoking in the rectory—I get it."

"You know the Hayley Mills rectory smoking scene! I can't believe it, I love that!"

"Let me open you a Coke and help yourself to the popcorn."

"And you love Lucy too!" I say.

"And Ethel, don't forget Ethel! We're on the same page when it comes to TV and movies. I'm a huge fan. I bet you've seen a lot in California. Did you ever go to Hollywood, being so close? I've always wanted to visit Hollywood," she says.

"Yah, several times actually. It's about seven hours away. Grauman's Chinese Theatre... all the foot and handprints. That makes me think of the Lucy episode where she and Ethel have to keep redoing John Wayne's square for the Theatre!"

"Oh, I love that one! Maybe it will be on one of these weeks. That would be cool to see it with you. Here's some tissue. I'm sorry to hear of everything you've been through," she says gently.

"Thanks, I don't know. It's been kind of a weird journey since I got the telegram about Trixie. I've just tried to put one foot in front of the other and keep going. And since I arrived on the island, it's been such a big change. Oh, you'll be interested in this, they're shooting a movie here on the island."

"A movie, here? That's big news, like from a real Hollywood studio?"

"Yes, I got a part as an extra. I'll be a maid who scrubs the floor and dusts. It's quite a big deal at the hotel, and they're trying to shoot a lot of the scenes with the big stars before most of the tourists arrive. It's starring Christopher Reeve, Jane Seymour, and Christopher Plummer and called *Somewhere in Time*. Trixie arranged for me to live at the Grand Hotel until the apartment above the store she left me can be made livable, so I'm looking to make some money to live on. That's part of the reason for stopping by. I thought you might need help with bingo-calling. I did it where we watched *I Love Lucy* when I got old enough."

"The movie sounds so exciting! I wish I could help you with a job, but we have a volunteer staff that runs the bingo. They earn free play cards, so there's always a waiting list. Oh look, *TV Guide* says it's the one where they stop in Ethel's hometown to see her Dad. Ethel gets to be a big deal in this one, I love that. I'm a big fan of Ethel."

"Ethel. I always think the name sounds like a type of gasoline. My Mom was a big Ethel fan, too, but she always struck me as someone who was just there to make sure Lucy could say her lines and look good," I say.

"Yah, it seems that way at a first look. But, really, I think we all can relate to Ethel, or maybe I should speak for myself. The world is attracted to Lucy, but I think most of us are walking around being Ethel and wondering why we're not the star. I've always been more intrigued by the people that other people don't seem to notice. I think that's how Jesus saw people too. Wait, does that bug you if I talk about

Jesus?" Sister asks.

And there it was. Catholic or Protestant, faith people always get around to talking about their faith. Listen, sister, you're not talking to a novice here, I know the score, I heard it every day. "To be honest, I don't know. I mean it's your place, you can say whatever you want. I was raised a Christian, but after everyone was killed, while they were out spreading the Gospel I might add, I quit faith. I've never said it out loud quite like that, but that's what happened, I lost my faith. Believe me, my dad was up to some stuff where I could justify what happened to him, but not my mom and my sister. Total innocents. I guess I came to a place where if that can be allowed by an all-knowing God, then maybe, He wasn't the one for me. That's pretty blasphemous talk from where I come from, but for some reason, I just want to be honest with someone finally. Wow, you're really not getting to see much *I Love Lucy* with me here are you?" I ask.

"Piper, it sounds like you've been through a lot in your life for a young lady. And losing your whole family, how painful. I'm sure you're not looking for advice from me, but, take it from someone who has not had an easy life either, I know what sustains me, keeps me joyful regardless of circumstances, and I know why I'm here. I would just like to be your friend, and if the time comes that you want to talk about those feelings you are having, I will listen. It might surprise you to know that from what I've studied about Jesus, he was not a fan of religion and manipulation. I've never known anyone who truly explored who He was, really took the time to read the Bible and try to understand Him with an open mind, to regret learning more," Sister says.

"Except that my whole life revolved around His teachings, and I'm not where you are. I'm sorry, I'm just being honest. I hope I don't offend you," I say.

"Please, be honest. And I can be honest too. I don't know if your thoughts about Jesus are based on your parents, or really knowing Him for yourself, because those could be two very different things. I know He loved each one of us enough to die for us, even if we never believed Him. I think you should read the book of John in the Bible for yourself. Read it in a more modern translation, one without the *thee's and thou's*. Or, if you choose not to, it's okay. I want to be your friend. You're fun, and we have a lot in common. So, if you want to talk about faith more, I'll leave it up to you. It's kind of my thing."

"It's just that I saw firsthand a man who claimed to believe and behind the scenes he lived a secret life that didn't match up. I stopped listening when the hypocrite in my own home became the bigger story to me. I'm sorry, you did not open your door to have all of this laid on you. Maybe I should just go."

"Are you kidding? What you need right now is popcorn and to see Ethel shine and laugh at Lucy. I'm thrilled that you knocked on my door. I'm only sorry that I can't help you with a job," Sister says. "But if it seems right to you, read the book of John with an open mind. I think you'll be surprised."

"I'll think about it, and yes, I'm ready for popcorn and some Ethel and Lucy. I don't know this episode very well. Thank you, Sister Mary-Margaret, thank you for, I don't know, caring, I guess."

She smiles at me, and we both burst out laughing at what Lucy did. Those expressions! I love how Lucy and Ethel took everyday situations and made them important. And, it was fun to eat popcorn and giggle with someone. Freddy was not exactly girlfriend material, and he was more distracting than anything, I had never seen this episode where Ethel was in the spotlight. Watching the credits, I couldn't believe it. A real nun and I sitting watching *I Love Lucy*, laughing and crying together—what an evening. These people on the island are very real. In just a couple of days I feel closer to a redhead and a nun than I felt to anyone for years in my hometown. It's a lot to take in. The show finishes very fast and I don't want to be a pest.

"Thanks again for inviting me in. I hope I didn't bring a cloud over your *I Love Lucy* time," I say.

"I do this every week, and I'd love it if you would join me, but don't feel as though you are obligated. I think we could have a lot of fun," she says.

"Really? Yes, I would like to. Thanks again. Next week, I'll pick up some fudge for a treat. Now, if I could use your phone, I can call a horse taxi to come and get me, one of the perks of living at the Grand for a few months."

"Sure, right over here. Help yourself."

We chat about all the nun clips from movies and TV that we have in common until the driver rings the bell to pick me up.

Clip clop. Clip clop. Listening to the rhythm of the horses taking me back to the Grand, seems to be the perfect background for all the thoughts swirling in my mind. But now Sister Mary-Margaret has added a layer of confusion! I don't know if I want to read the book of John. Maybe I'm afraid she is right. I mean, it feels fine to be where I am, it makes sense to me. I was taught a bunch of stuff I don't believe anymore. It's part of being an adult, you must figure out what is right for you, not just go on what your parents believed. But what she said set something off in me. What if I've been wallowing in my misery so long, I'm not open to anything? She seems so sure and all I've known lately is uncertainty.

Redheads are changing my world, first Lucy, then Cam. And I think I saw something peeking out of her habit—a tiny red curl! I'm sensing a theme, and it frightens and thrills me all at the same time. *Read the book of John in a modern version*, that's what she said. I've heard about them, and it must be better than the Bibles I grew up with. The Bibles I've read are even more confusing than the Transatlantic dialect as far as I'm concerned.

Okay. Tomorrow I'll get a Bible if I can and start to read it. At least, when I see Sister for the next *I Love Lucy* episode, I won't have to lie if she asks if I read it or not. She's way too young to be my mother, but she has that thing that feels like an old soul wrapping a warm blanket around my heart. Being with her was comforting, like a parent who cares, like my mom. It's been so long since I was able to feel that, and I miss it. I'll read enough of the Bible to not be lying if she asks me. I can skim it and then I will not be deceiving her. Like when I got the CliffsNotes for a book in school so I could pass the test without reading the book. Maybe old Cliff could get me by with Sister when it comes to John. Then again, trying to trick a nun about reading the Bible…

Yes, I've still got it. Maybe I just got caught up in the evening. I don't know, living in San Fran wasn't the worse thing. I did fine. Maybe these people are screwed up, and I see things clearly. I don't want to buy into some big false hope again. In San Fran I was in control. This is all over the place and I have to be more careful about this island seduction. That's it. These people are seducing me, and then real life is going to smack me in the face, and I'll feel worse than ever. I don't know these people; I'm being too vulnerable. My big mistake wasn't stealing, it was getting caught.

If you're going to be a villain, be a good one.

Grow up, Piper. This isn't make-believe. I'll read enough of John to get by, I'm an expert at getting by. To think I was almost sucked into all of this.

Put me in front of Lucy and give me some munchies and I'll believe anything. Well, as they say, Sister, fool me once.

Chapter Nine

∼⚭∼

I hate a tossing-and-turning night, and this is a doozy. I might as well get up even though it's before seven. I'll just get dressed and head down to the dining room for early breakfast. I love living here, but I really am out of my element. These people have money. No one else could quite afford the time here without a nice bank account. I didn't come equipped to be dressing for dinner every night, which is mandatory. All men and ladies are required to be attired in their finest after 6 p.m., as the various reminders throughout the hotel clearly state. One denim and one black skirt and a shawl have hardly cut it in the fashion department. It's time to shake it up.

Thankfully, the shop here in the Grand has taken my small watercolor paintings, and they seem to be selling well. At least I feel I can breathe a little with my pennies. Everyone who comes here wants a souvenir of the beauty to take home. And because most people here have some bucks, the shop has put a price on each postcard-size painting far beyond what I would ever think would be possible to get. It's time to get a few more basic pieces of clothes that will work well for the evening meal. I'm thinking the concierge can point me to some shops in town that will help. Wait! There's a semi-familiar face. I don't know what she's doing here in the lobby, but she is a good person to ask.

"Miss Fields! Miss Fields!" I never did catch her first name when I was at the law office. I might have to yell louder with her on the other side of the lobby. Man, she's fast. Oh good, she's looking my way.

"Oh, hello, Miss Penn, just one of my many runs to drop off paperwork here at the hotel. As the only lawyers in town, there's always something to deliver to the hotel owners, or the businesspeople here for vacation. So nice to see you, but I'm in a hurry, always so much to do," Miss Fields says. She turns and starts to leave.

"Wait, can I just ask you a quick question? I'm wondering if you could recommend a dress shop in town for people our age, something affordable, maybe even secondhand?" I ask.

"You didn't live a dress-up life in San Francisco, now did you? I mean people on the street there dress like hobos! Yes, it's a little different here at the Grand. Here's what you do—go to Molly's on Main. She has gorgeous clothes and some gently worn items too. Molly's on Main, you can't miss it!"

And, she's gone. For such a relaxing, tranquil atmosphere, the locals always seem to be in a hurry. Perfect. I'll follow up with Cam's idea to meet the Conrad brothers at my shop and apartment—my shop, my apartment, it still sounds so odd. After that I'll head to Molly's for some clothes, probably a basic black dress if I can find one. Maybe another scarf or shawl. That way I can dress it up differently throughout the week. I wouldn't mind looking a little nicer when I run into Mr. Red. Maybe we'll even have dinner sometime. After all, a girl's gotta be seen in more than jeans and a T-shirt occasionally.

But first, I want to go and explore the labyrinth below the Grand Hotel in the small woods. I can't see it from the porch, but the map in my room shows it to be below the hotel, beyond the pool, settled in the woods. I've always wanted to see a labyrinth. My mom told me the story growing up of a neighbor who went to a famous labyrinth at the Chartres Cathedral in France. I remember the look of pure wonder on my mom's face when she told me how the monks used it for contemplative prayer since the year 1205. The way she said it with a whisper, I wanted to remember every detail, including the year. Her eyes always got a little misty when she talked about it as if she could see herself there. She said she wanted to experience it sometime. I could tell it felt sacred to her. Maybe I'll find something at this labyrinth or feel closer to her. Heading across the porch and down the stairs, I have those same feelings of excitement I used to get at the library as I scoped out my next *Nancy Drew* mystery. I couldn't wait to escape into that world. Okay, down the steps, across the lawn, around the pool... I want to give a shout every time I walk in the pool area and say, "Hello, Esther Williams!" but I restrain myself. There's the small entrance break in the woods. This is lovely, a small plaque near the narrow opening announces me to the labyrinth. Cool sign.

It talks about walking a sacred path, and quiet meditation. Interesting. This version it says resembles a labyrinth that was constructed in the twelfth century at Chartres Cathedral in France.

My pulse is racing. The very one my mom talked about so reverently is mentioned at this labyrinth, too. This gives me goosebumps. Stepping through the opening I see it—the twists and turns of a path that leads to a center, all done with small green plants and stones. Hello, labyrinth. I could use some peace.

All right, feet. Start at the beginning and follow to the center. Wait. I'm supposed to pray, not just admire the foliage. I haven't prayed in forever. Not really prayed. "God bless this grub" in front of Frap doesn't count. Deep breaths, Mom said. Feet together. Close your eyes and bow your head, Piper. I hear the quiet, a slight breeze in the trees, and the soft sound of the water lapping on the shore in the distance. Go forward, stay in the path. Being here, I feel some of the snarky attitude constantly cloaking my life falling off a bit, and oh boy, here come the tears.

I remember. I remember Jesus, loving you. Believing in you. Knowing that you know the very hairs on my head. I remember a verse about all things working together for my good. I'm still so confused, but I'm willing to try to understand. Amen.

That's all I can handle right now. Keep moving, stay in the path. I remember. Jesus, you sent the Holy Spirit to be the Comforter. Comfort, something I have not known since I was very little, too small to understand anything. I do feel something, and maybe it's peace. This feels real and surreal all at the same time. I don't want to push this all away because of fear. I don't want to be this person I've become who always expects the worst and waits for bad things to happen.

I don't want to be someone who would disappoint my mom.

So many thoughts and here I am, already in the center of the labyrinth. I get now why my mother whispered when she spoke about it. I never understood, really understood the word 'sacred' before. This feels sacred. Walking back out of the labyrinth, I do know what's next.

I'm going to start a new journal entry. This is why I'm glad I always have my satchel with me, filled with my journal, sketchbook, my small watercolors, and my handy-dandy binoculars. I never got to be a Girl Scout, but this girl is prepared. I think the girls with the badges would be proud. This bench next to the labyrinth is perfect. I'm ready. I should do my regular style of journaling, and George Burns, who so famously played God, would be the perfect person to write to, but I can't go that far, even if it's just me and paper. I must be real.

Dear God,

We used to be close, but I'm having a hard time even going there again. I feel bad about that, I remember the lessons about "If you don't feel close to God anymore, He's not the one who moved." But after four years, I'm getting even more scared about not talking to you. I remember when I believed in The Trinity, when you three made sense to me. The Father, the Son, and Holy

Spirit. But seeing my dad through the years, the pain he brought into our family and then how it ripped my heart out to lose them all. Was that really the only way? But I did have the thought, maybe an epiphany really, that Jesus's death was the way we reconnect back to your Holiness, God. Jesus even asked if there was another way in the garden of Gethsemane, He wasn't crazy about the pain either. I wonder, how could my dad, who claimed to know Jesus so well, become this person at our house? How am I, someone who saw behind the scenes of the pretty words, supposed to believe in an all-knowing, all-loving God who allows so many horrors? Remember, God, after they died, and I went to talk to a pastor at that church? He said that humans are flawed and always have choices—including living the truth. It was also pointed out to me that Jesus, and the rest of the Holy Trinity, were really the only ones I can use as my litmus test. People would fail me, Jesus would not. Even if I thought He was failing me, He never was. I've been so raw and hurt. Getting out of San Francisco for the first time has given me some perspective, I think. To be truthful, I don't know how much I've ever read the Bible for myself. I was born into it—it was always just there—and shoved down my throat. My depth of learning doesn't go much past the flannel characters the teachers used in Sunday School, like Moses, Noah, and David and Goliath. "Accept Jesus as my Savior"—that's what we were told—"and we would be saved." I was saved possibly hundreds of times if you count confessing my sins and going up to an altar to repent. There—Heaven, done. What does dying and going to Heaven really mean to a pastor's kid and how many times can you repent from not making your bed in the morning, or that you stole a soda out of the fridge? I don't know if I've ever really known you and I don't know if I want to. Even thinking like that makes me want to step aside from the lightning bolt I imagine is coming my way. But maybe, Lord, I've confused you with a genie in a bottle. The more I write, the more confused I am. I will say this. I think there's a reason I met Sister Mary-Margaret. She must know a lot, and she seems real and not fake. I need clarity. I need to know. Please help me find you.

Very, very sincerely,
Piper
P.S. I am sorry for stealing. It started out as a thrill to see what I could get away with and it helped numb the pain from losing my family. I kept stealing because I needed things and I didn't have much money. I stole art supplies. I knew it was wrong, and I'm sorry. Please forgive me.

Time has stood still in the woods near the labyrinth, something that happens to me when I'm lost in journaling. More deep breaths. Part of me wants to stay in this moment and just be still, but the real world is calling me back. I better get going.

So I keep my appointment for the estimate from the Conrad brothers, and then to Molly's for a dress. I should be thinking of practicality, something that will go with everything, but all I can think about is something that will wow a certain redhead. But before those stops, I have an even more important place to be.

Chapter Ten

Christopher Reeve and Jane Seymour spent most of the day walking by me as their movie characters while I was down on my knees scrubbing a baseboard. If I had a line in the movie, I would be paid more, but no such luck. I simply scrub as they walk by saying their lines repeatedly. I'm one step above lint on the floor playing this role, but I get a little money, and I can say I was in a movie. The assistant to the assistant of the director did mention that I might get to dress up for one of the dining room scenes. After a long morning on my knees, the last thing I want to do is go to a meeting, but it's mandatory for the cast. At least I might get to say 'hi' to Cam. With his job, and his part as an extra, he doesn't have much time to hang out.

"Hey, scrub lady, how's it going?" Cam and I flow with the rest of the crew and cast walking down the stairs toward the meeting room.

"I could use some knee pads. How do you do all that flower weeding and not have knee aches?" I ask.

"Calluses. You get used to it. Praying and weeding. I'm conditioned," Cam says.

"Praying? Well, say some of those for me. Pray me up a million bucks so I can get my store up and running. The Conrad brothers seem like great guys but the list of repairs they gave me had my eyes rolling in my head, nothing personal against them. Repairs are expensive!"

"That's part of being on an island and shipping everything here, the costs really go up. I'll get together with them and go over the list, to make sure we are being as frugal as we can. Maybe I can help out more."

"Are you kidding? You don't even have time to eat as it is… so I don't see you taking on a construction project too. I'm sure their price is fair, but truthfully, I know nothing about construction."

"Let's see what I can do. I'll go over their plans with them just to make sure we are getting the bang for the buck."

"Well, I would like to know it's being done right, so thank you. Hey, I went to the labyrinth. I bet you planted it. I love it there, so peaceful. And a good place to elude the fudgies."

"Ah, you're not feeling like you're a fudgie, huh? Got that 'I'm not one of those tourists, I'm one of the islanders' vibe going, I like it," Cam jokes. "Yes, the labyrinth is one of my favorite projects. For some reason, it's not a top spot for the tourists to hit, so it's often empty, which is fine by me. And, I'm not gonna lie, my crew and I do a lot of hard work to set it up every year and make it look nice. So, I am proud of the outcome too."

"Well, I loved it. I can see myself going there often."

I'm also loving the smile I see on Cam's face right now. Taking our seats for the meeting, I'm still surprised by how many behind-the-scenes people it takes to get a movie made.

"Let's quiet, people, I don't want to take more of your time than is necessary." The assistant to the assistant director is at the front of the room. "We have a town person here, who would like to say a few words. Please give your attention to Katherine Sims-Dubois, town chairwoman of the board here on the island."

Katherine emerges from a dark corner where none of us had noticed her as we filed into the meeting.

"Oh great, the queen gets her fingers into everything she can—if I knew she was here, I wouldn't have come." Cam leans over and whispers in my ear.

"Thank you, sir, it's my pleasure on behalf of the Mackinac Island Town Board to welcome you all to our amazing island," Katherine says. "If there is anything we can do to make your stay more comfortable, please don't hesitate to ask. I want to let you know that all our fine shops want to offer you a twenty percent discount during your stay, so be sure to stop in. Just say you're with the movie, and you'll get the discount. You'll all want souvenirs from your time here in paradise. If you need anything, my office door downtown at the town board headquarters is always open, so welcome, welcome, welcome!"

Starting the clapping to get the crowd to join in, the assistant returns to the front of the room.

"A reminder to pay attention to your schedule and don't be late, time is money here, people. Next, uh, just a minute, folks."

The assistant stops talking abruptly. The assistant director, one step up in the movie food chain, is making his way to the front of the room and I, like the rest of the room, am looking around to see what's up. None of us have much contact with him, and never the director. We were warned in the beginning to keep our distance beyond a 'hello', and to forget the idea of approaching him about being in any of his upcoming movies. Seems we extras tend to think alike.

"Hi, guys and gals," the assistant director says. "I want to thank all of you for the important part you play to make this a very big hit. Everyone matters. We do have a troubling incident I want to bring to your attention. There's been some theft of some of the jewelry being used in the movie and you can understand how disturbing this is."

At this news, heads turn throughout the room and people start whispering. It sounds like a hive of bees was just let loose. My palms are sweating, and that's putting it politely. They're pouring water. This can't be happening.

"We think we have an idea as to who might be responsible, but if you have seen anything that you think might be helpful to our investigation, please speak with your segment's assistant. We want to nip this type of thing in the bud, and I hope no one in this room had anything to do with this. We need to trust each other. There's too much to do to have something like this happen," the assistant director says.

The murmuring is ramping up. Everyone wants to tell someone sitting near them their theory on what could have happened.

"That's crazy, who would do something so stupid?" Cam whispers.

"I know, I can't imagine," I whisper back.

I hope he doesn't notice how flushed my face is right now.

"Mr. Director! Mr. Director!" Katherine Sims-Dubois is trying to be heard above the din.

"Ma'am, I'm the assistant director and I didn't realize we had non-cast people here," he says passing a dirty look to his assistant.

"Wouldn't you want to look first at people who have a history of theft in their background? That would make the most sense," Mrs. Dubois says.

She's looking right at me, and my face must be getting even redder than before. A verse I heard as a kid comes to my mind—"be sure your sins will find you out."

"Of course, we'll be exploring every angle, but this is an internal matter, which we feel more than adequate to handle on our own, so thank you for your concern," the assistant director says, clearly irritated that Katherine is butting in.

"But I happen to know of a cast member with a history of theft!" Mrs. Dubois starts to yell excitedly. "There's a thief among us!"

Katherine is heading right for me and I don't know what to do.

Chapter Eleven

"Mrs. Dubois, is it? Please! Please!" the assistant director bellows.

The room has gone crazy with loud whispers of people putting out theories of something they think they saw.

"I won't name names, but someone's brother is in jail downstate for theft, and it's well known that he was part of it but got out of the conviction. Even though he's a relative, I can't stand by and let this happen," Mrs. Dubois says coming to a dead stop at the row where I sit next to Cam. "It's a family of ne'er-do-wells and we simply can't have that strain on our pristine island community. I've worked too hard for this island."

I'm almost pushed off my chair from Cam jumping up so fast. He brushes past me to get to Mrs. Dubois. His face is so red, it matches his hair. He gets right in her face, yelling loudly, and I wonder if he's going to punch her!

"If you're referring to my family, Katherine, back off! I have never stolen anything in my life—ever. Obviously, you've lost your mind, and your hate for my family has caused you to embarrass yourself." Cam storms past her and out of the room.

"That's enough, Mrs. Dubois. We will handle this. Cam is not under any suspicion, and, everyone, stop with the gossip. If you have something helpful to say, speak only to your segment assistant," the assistant director shouts over the noisy room.

I can't move.

Glaring at the assistant director, Katherine fluffs her skirt and huffs, inciting even more whispers in the room.

Oh my gosh, Cam! I feel so bad for you, but the truth is, I also feel relieved she doesn't know about my past. She sure has it out for Cam and his family. Why does she hate him so much? I thought for sure she was on to me and calling me out. I didn't steal any jewelry, but with my past, I could easily be a suspect. At least she must not have an insider in the police department.

Even though everyone is gone, I feel frozen to my chair. Here I am, dressed like a scrub maid, soaked in sweat from head to toe from all the drama, and all I can think about is how long it will be before she does find out about my past. What kind of trouble can she cause for me? Maybe she can even invoke a board vote against my inheritance. Who knows what's possible after what I just saw? I need to get to my room, get a shower, get a meal, and get my bearings back. And I thought scrubbing on my knees was going to be the low point of my day. Room 308, my sanctuary, here I come. Stand up. Good. Progress. Oh no, I hear that swishing skirt again. She's back, and she hasn't calmed down one bit.

"Miss Penn!" Katherine is way too close in my comfort zone of personal space. "Next time you see your boyfriend, tell him his family will not be allowed to put a stain on our family name and perhaps he should be seeking employment anywhere but on our blessed island. You tell him that, young lady!"

Her body is shaking, and she is spitting in my face as she talks. Suddenly, the Transatlantic accent is gone, and the real deal is emerging.

"Katherine, calm down! First, Cam is not my boyfriend, he's a colleague. Secondly, he is an individual. He is not his siblings or his parents, so I don't understand why you are so upset about his presence here. He doesn't even work on Main Street. He's here at the Grand, so you don't need to see him at all," I say.

I can't believe I'm confronting her.

"It's not for you to know everything, young missy, you're not blood, but let Mr. Redhead know that if he wants to make any trouble for me, he doesn't know who he is dealing with. Any threats he wants to throw my way will not be taken lightly. No one threatens me without retaliation," she says.

"Has Cam threatened you? What are you talking about?" I ask.

"Just let him know I'm watching him. I don't appreciate cut-and-paste threatening notes shoved under my door, and I won't put up with it!"

Katherine pokes me in the shoulder with her finger, emphasizing her point. Then, as if she put her evil twin back in her pocket, she collects her composure right before my very eyes and gets back to her usual dripping demeanor. Stepping back finally, I'm thankful the spitting has stopped with every *p* and *t* she uttered.

"Now then, that's that." Oh joy, her accent is back. "Nothing personal, I hope you are getting along fine here. I also hope you won't hold these family issues against me, but I would appreciate it if you would deliver my message, since I can't seem to get him to take a message. Have a nice day," Katherine says.

And with that and the usual swish of her skirt, she turns and leaves.

"Katherine, I can't promise I'll even see Cam…"

She didn't hear me. Thankfully, no one else is nearby to witness this craziness. Oh room 308, if I can just get there. My knees hurt, I smell like a scrub bucket, and all this drama is exhausting. I should be able to use the workers' elevator and avoid most of the tourists. Pressing the elevator button over and over doesn't make it arrive any faster, but it makes me feel better.

I wonder who is stealing the jewelry. So many beautiful pieces that Jane Seymour's character wears in her role, not to mention all the dress-up scenes needing jewelry. It could be anyone. Did the thief really think that no one would notice? And why is Katherine so freaked out by Cam? As far as I can see, he can't stand her and wants nothing to do with her. I also have a feeling that if I mention my encounter with her to Cam he might take it as an accusation from me. I never saw him lose his temper like he did when she accused him, but then, who wouldn't in that scene? What did she mean by notes under a door? All these thoughts are making my head hurt even more.

Finally, my room. Sanctuary, sanity, and bubbles galore in a moment except now there's knocking on my door. Can't I just be left alone for five minutes, please! I secure my robe, I answer it.

"A note for you, my lady."

Oh good, another closed note. I close the door and open the note.

Dear Piper,

Can you meet me at 3 p.m. in the labyrinth? There's something you need to know. If you don't want to see me, I'll understand, but I'll be there if you're available.

Sincerely,

Cam

I'm glad I get to see him. He was so upset, and I hope he doesn't feel bad on my account. Okay, bath, you just became a quick shower. Of course, I want to see you, Cam. And, why am I so excited to spend time with him? Rein it in, Piper. Everyone here has some kind of secret. Be careful.

Chapter Twelve

"I wasn't sure you would come." Cam stands up from the bench. I wonder if he's been waiting long, which isn't a chore here in the labyrinth.

"Cam, I'm so sorry about what happened. It was unfair, and weird, and I don't even know how to describe adequately how awful it must have felt for you getting blindsided like that," I say.

"Oh man, talk about embarrassing, and in front of some people on my staff. And, she said all of that in front of the assistant director… and you," Cam says.

"Don't worry about me. But, Cam, she's bat-crazy! She came back to the room after everyone was gone. I was alone and she went off on a tangent again about you and your family. She asked me to tell you that she's watching you. How did she put it—any threats you want to throw her way will not be taken lightly, and she said something about passing notes under the door. Did you give her a note?"

"A note? I would not write a note to that weirdo. No, I have no idea what that means. No notes, I want to stay as far away from her as possible. If I didn't love it here and my job, I'd hightail it off this island. When I took the job here, she put on a big, over-the-top welcome, like some prodigal was coming back to the fold. When I snubbed her, she got snotty and abrasive, but that's where it stopped. We just stayed out of each other's way and that was that. But the explosion we just witnessed, that was something else, that was freaky." Cam puts his face in his hands.

I want to hug him so bad, but a small back-pat seems right. I hate to see him hurting.

"Yah, she said the note was cut-out pasted letters, like old ransom notes in old movies," I say.

"Honestly, she is so delusional, I wouldn't put it past her making up the note to cause more drama or cause a scene on purpose."

"Cam, is it worth a one-on-one conversation with her to just get to the bottom of this and stop it once and for all? Maybe you can agree to disagree and leave each other alone?" I ask softly.

"I don't know, I can't stand her—bringing my brother into this. He's no saint, I'll admit, but he got in with the wrong crowd. We're not a close family, but he's doing the time for what he did. I hope when he gets out, he'll grow up and live right. Our parents passed in a car accident a few years ago, and that goofed us all up. We all just went our own ways, and maybe when I get my act together, I can help him. I'm the baby of the family so they don't tend to listen to me."

"Your parents were both killed? Oh my gosh, Cam, I do know how you feel, and I lost my twin sister too. They were all killed in Africa when their hut was set on fire."

Tears again? Why am I crying again? I was so much better at keeping it together in San Francisco. There are tears in his eyes too. We hug. Tightly. A long hug, as if for the first time since this happened, I'm getting comfort from someone who matters—someone who knows the depth of this never-ending pain. His shirt is soft against my cheek, and I smell the geranium soap which is so popular at the Grand. I don't want this hug to ever end but we both jump at the same time.

"Did you hear that too? Leaves rustling?" Cam asks.

"I can't see beyond these perimeter trees. Squirrels maybe?" I ask.

"Probably a squirrel or two, could even be a fox. The woods have lots of hidden critters," Cam says.

"You know them better than I do, I'm just a jumpy city girl. But, really, Cam, what do you think about talking to Katherine?"

"Right now, I'm much more interested in your story. I didn't realize we were both orphans."

"The orphan club... the few, the proud."

Sitting here with Cam, in this sacred setting on this island, I want him to know me, the real me. For the first time since my family passed, I am spilling out everything about my past. I tell the whole sordid story including the way my Dad treated us, how he was rising to fame, the loneliness, the stealing—everything. I tell him about being mad at myself, and God.

"Hmm, on the outs with God, huh? Maybe I should scoot over to the end of this bench," Cam says.

I love his sense of humor, and how he knows just when to lighten up the moment.

"I'm just exploring Jesus for myself," he says. "I wasn't raised with the whole idea. My parents weren't really anything. I started to read about Buddhism, but it didn't add up for me. I think Jesus is interesting and real. I'm reading a Bible, something I've never done. And, I've started praying. That's why I like the labyrinth. I use it to slow down and concentrate on a daily prayer. In fact, before I deal with my crazy cousin, I might just do some praying first. Can't hurt."

"I'm reading the Bible too! Well, sort of. I've become friends with a nun at St. Anne's, Sister Mary-Margaret. We bonded over *I Love Lucy*, and she challenged me to read if for myself. But she said to do it in a modern version, not the *thee's* and *thou's* kind of Bible I grew up with."

"I get that," Cam says. "I made sure to get something that I could understand. It's hard enough to read without feeling like I'm hanging out with Shakespeare or something. We should compare notes. I don't know anyone else reading the Bible to talk to about it."

"I just picked up it recently at that little bookstore downtown," I reply. "I don't want to disappoint her because she's fun to hang out with, but truthfully, I haven't given it too much attention yet, so you're way ahead of me. But, back to the crazy meeting, do you see why I was inwardly freaking out when Katherine was coming toward us? I thought she was coming to expose me. Saying that out loud in front of you makes me sound like a narcissist."

"Well, then, maybe there's a silver lining. I would rather have her come after me than you. Quit being so hard on yourself."

We jump again at the same time because this rustling is not squirrels.

"Cam! That was not animals in the woods. Someone has been eavesdropping—those were footsteps! Someone just heard everything, including the fact that I stole. My life story, my secrets…" I'm going to cry. Again. This could make me lose everything.

"What creep eavesdrops on people like that? Maybe it would be a good idea for you to go back to your room, Piper. I'm gonna see if I can catch this person," Cam says, taking off after the eavesdropper.

Cam is right. What kind of person hides in a woods and listens in on a conversation? Was it Katherine or one of her moles? She says she knows everything that happens on this island. All I can think about as I head back is that someone else has information about me that could wreck my life, and someone is out to get me or Cam. Or maybe both of us.

Chapter Thirteen

I'm dying to hear from Cam, but I know if he has any news, he would tell me. He did stop at my door later to let me know he didn't catch anyone. Standing there, looking up at him, I didn't want him to leave. My heart was racing, and we whispered to one another, getting closer and closer to each other. I was shivering, and it wasn't from the cold. With him, I feel like I belong somehow, or a connection. This is the life I've seen in the movies, but nothing I've ever experienced. It didn't hurt that he gave me a sweet short kiss and a hug as he said good night. That felt calming after my mind went wild with who was listening in the woods—at least enough so I could get some sleep before all the thoughts returned this morning. Plus, I appreciate that he's busy and I don't want to be one more problem for him.

I'm glad it's *I Love Lucy* night with Sister Mary-Margaret. Since the running footsteps in the labyrinth yesterday, I'm out of sorts. It's like those horrible moments in a scary movie waiting for something to jump out and scare you to death. Everyone I see in the parlor looks like they could be the person who was listening to our conversation. I now understand paranoia. It's good I'm having dinner in my room, and doubly good the hotel offers it as a service. At least all this drama is helpful for the waistline. I don't feel like eating, but if I don't, I get shaky, and I'm having enough of that right now. Skipping dressing for dinner is also a relief. I want to wear my new black dress when I know I'll see Cam. I'll snack a little, just enough to quiet my nerves, and try some deep breathing. I want to enjoy my walk to the rectory at St. Anne's in my jeans and T-shirt. It's a bit of a hike, but I need the exercise. I need to get off the Grand grounds and feel some space.

Heading out, I see the Straits are calm, no action from Lake Michigan or Lake Huron to make it wavy. Round Island Lighthouse looks peaceful with a slight mist. The lake does have its own personality. Some days the waves are gigantic, especially when the wind picks up. Being here, I can see why there have been so many shipwrecks in these Great Lakes. I remember the wreck of the *Edmund Fitzgerald* a few years ago. Even though it was Lake Superior, I get how big these waves can be. Every time Gordon Lightfoot's "Wreck of the Edmund Fitzgerald" came on the radio I would turn it up very loud, and now I feel even closer to the song. I've almost worn out his *Summertime Dream* cassette that has the song. I feel related in some way to these mammoth bodies of water, and I want to go and see all of them. The ocean is something, but these lakes have a drama all their own. Today has been calm, which is good. The freighters can travel in peace. I love watching them pass by majestically when I paint in my room. I think about the people on the boat, and the unique life they are living.

Earlier today from my balcony, I could see they were doing a movie scene out by Round Island Lighthouse with Jane and Christopher. I love my new binoculars, one of my best purchases here on the island. They give me a closer look at the island's curiosities. Birds, the long freighters and various size boats, interesting tourists, it's an enjoyable pastime to sit in the Grand and watch the world go by. It looked like a romantic scene from what I could see. We don't get to read the whole script as extras, only the scene we are in. Many of us are trying to piece the story together from each other's pages. The movie is probably not even close to some of the ideas we have. My room and my little balcony open the world to me. I get to see the beauty, what's happening, and I have sanctuary all at the same time.

Walking by these gnarly lilac trees ready to burst into purple beauty, I want to paint them even more than I already have. They are one of my main subjects at this time of year. I sat near a local at a coffee shop last week and listened in on his version of how the trees were brought to the island. I had heard talk of them coming from France, but this person disagreed. He said it was the settlers in the early nineteenth century who came from New England. They brought the plants right along with their furniture, a piece of home. Soon everyone wanted lilacs around their summer cottages. That's what started this lilac saga from his point of view. I have found that the locals love to be the "informant" on all things island to anyone who seems curious. Fine with me, I can't get enough.

Clip clop, clip clop. That sound never gets old. From the hackneys to the Dutch Friesians, the variety and breeds of horses never cease to amaze me. They are magnificent to behold and seem to understand their duty to the island when they arrive each spring to begin their work. Maybe I've seen *Black Velvet* too many times, but each one has a striking personality that comes through their gorgeous big eyes. Dogs barking, kids laughing and playing before they get called in for the night. The lake breeze on my face. Bicyclists whooshing by, and some going at a leisurely pace. Either they are taking in the sights, or maybe they aren't used to all the biking that happens here. And, the sweet smell of the fudge shops. The horns blowing, signaling the ferries are on their way, taking the tourists back to the mainland. What a serene, lovely place—especially if you haven't screwed up your life. And now, St. Anne's. This majestic white beauty, the image of a small-town church. I need the distraction of the good sister, and the crazy Lucy and Ethel so much right now. I do love these walks from the Grand to St. Anne's.

"Hi, Piper, Welcome! I've been looking forward to our evening all day." Sister Mary-Margaret greets me at the side door to the rectory. I'm still astounded. I'm hanging out with a nun and we're watching *I Love Lucy* reruns.

"Did you have a good week? Any progress on your place?" she asks.

"It was an interesting week, let's put it that way. There was some jewelry theft on the set, and they haven't caught the person yet, so everyone is still a suspect," I say.

"What? That's sad to hear, and disturbing. I hope they catch the thief. We don't want our island to get a bad reputation in the movie community—it's not good for tourism."

"I know. It's put a bit of a damper on the set for us peons, especially since no one was caught. I feel like everyone looks at each other weirdly since they brought it up. And yes, to answer your question about my place, I think I have a crew to get started and do a good job. Do you know Cam, the groundskeeper at the Grand?"

"No, I don't know too many people who don't come to church because I'm kept so busy here. Honestly, I might have met him, but it's the church people who I really remember the most. But that's wonderful that you got an answer. I was praying that you would."

"Oh… yah… well thanks for that."

"Sorry, I said I would leave any faith talks up to you, but I didn't think you would mind me praying. I pray about everything and for everyone I care about. I don't believe in coincidence. I think God directs every step I take, and that includes every person I meet. So, how could I not talk to Him about your need?" she says with a giggle.

I love to hear Mary-Margaret giggle. It's never embarrassment, or tense. It's a sound of pure joy that comes from the tip of her toes and feels like liquid sunshine. If I could drink her giggles I would. They calm me and make me happy. Jesus knew what He was doing when he picked her to be his Midwest ambassador.

"Honestly, Mary-Margaret, if there's anyone I would like to talk to about faith, it would be you. And, I did go to the labyrinth at the Grand, and I had a prayer moment, it felt, well, sacred. I prayed. I took your suggestion and picked up a modern version of the Bible. I've looked at it a little bit so far, starting in John. But I'm still stuck on what has happened to me. The very person that was supposed to be so close to God, my dad—and mind you, he knew the Bible backwards and forwards—was abusing my mother. He was a horrible dad to us kids most of the time and maybe he was even having an affair. I see hints of that in my mother's diaries. And, then to top it off, my mom and sister are killed because of a decision he made. They went to please him, went to a very dangerous part of Africa which was like a publicity stunt to get more attention and TV time. How does all that add up to a loving God who would allow that to happen?" I ask, trying to squelch the high pitch as my voice elevates, and I feel my anger rising.

"I hear you, Piper, and you're not alone in that tough question. Why doesn't God prevent the death of so many innocents when so many wicked people prosper and seem to get even more? That's one of the questions everyone comes to in their life, although not as violently and as young as when you have had to face this. Even though it's hard, I'm still happy that our God gave us free will. He didn't want children who would have to love Him, be forced to love Him. He wanted children who would understand the sacrifice He made in sending His Son to die for the sins of everyone. Anyone who chooses to believe that and chooses to live in Christ in a true and authentic way is promised not only eternal life, but peace and a relationship during life here. So, it starts with the verse John 3:16... I imagine you know that verse," she says.

"Yes, that's one I can say by heart. *For God so loved the world that he gave his only begotten Son, that whosoever believes in Him will not perish, but will have everlasting life.* I feel like I'm a kid again at vacation Bible school. That's a verse we all had to memorize."

"That's where the relationship starts, but it doesn't stop there. Your dad began there at some point in his life, but somewhere on his journey, probably when fame came along, he wasn't making the right choices when it came to living in Christ. It says in I Peter 5:8, *Be alert and of sober mind. Your enemy the devil prowls around like a roaring lion looking for someone to devour.* So, we all have an enemy, the essence of pure evil, who actively is always trying to trip us up. He is always seeing who he can destroy, and obviously, he wants to destroy Christians, effective Christians, more than anyone. I can't judge your dad, but the evidence of his actions points to his choice to turn away from living in Christ as Jesus intended. And, the consequences have been horrific. But that was never the plan for his life. And now, you want black and white, complete answers based on your suffering. But, that's just not how life works. There's a much bigger picture and story happening," she says.

"I guess I'm kind of a baby... I'm starting to see that I talk about myself a lot, it's all me, me, me lately. Let's add that to the loser pile—selfish."

"Piper, would you really want to worship an all-sovereign, knowing, loving God who, instead of fulfilling the ultimate goals of your life from His viewpoint, instead makes decisions based on your finite mind in the moment? I think it was C.S. Lewis who pointed out that even Jesus didn't have a prayer answered the way He initially wanted it to be. In the garden He prayed that 'this cup would pass from me.'"

"It's really weird you would say that because I had that same thought when I was trying to pray in the labyrinth, the thought that Jesus did ask for what was going to happen to Him to be taken away if possible."

"You did? Oh, I love to hear how God is working. There are no coincidences, Piper."

"My mom used to say that too!"

"I think your mom and I would have been great friends. It's true. Jesus knew the gut-wrenching agony He was going to have to bear to take on the sins of the whole world, all so they—and that includes you and me—would be able to be with the Father for eternity if we chose to. He knew it was going to ask far more of Him than anything ever had. But he didn't end the prayer there, which if it was me, I probably would have. He continued and said to His Father—I want what You see needs to happen, or as it says: 'Thy will be done'. And that was His ultimate ask. He said, here's what I'm hoping and thinking, but ultimately, God, you know the end result. I trust You that You know what should happen, so that's what I really want. I know we're getting really deep here, and I hope it's not turning you off, but the question becomes, can you and I pray like that to a God who wants to hear our thoughts, but also wants our trust that He knows best and knows our story from start to eternity? That's a big question, but one we have to think about."

"Sister Mary-Margaret, you make my brain hurt, but in a good way. I've never thought about these things quite like this. But, honestly, I'm not sure I want to."

"Well, you have a light inside of you that makes me smile, even if I make your brain hurt! Piper, your personal choices are yours. What your dad did or didn't do isn't your faith walk. And, here's something that may be hard for you to hear, but you have no idea what happened between your dad and God in that hut. It's entirely possible that he asked for forgiveness and saw the error of the direction he had taken. I don't have an answer for you as to why God didn't just stop the fire, because He could have, and let them all come home to you. But I do know that as it says in Romans 8:28, all things work together for the good for those who love God. It's not an easy thing to believe on our own. We need faith like a child and to trust that things are going to work out in the best way possible in the big picture. Without faith, we will keep judging God on a list of what we think He did right, and what we think He did wrong. Since we see such a small snippet of a whole story, can we really be the best choice to call the shots in comparison to an all-seeing, all-knowing, loving God?"

"That's an interesting way to put it. Heaven knows I like to be in charge. Oh, my gosh, what I just said!"

"You're funny. But, here's my bottom-line, Piper. If you can't honestly say that you have explored the Word of God with an open heart to understand who He is *to you*, and tried to understand why He would sacrifice His Son *for you*, then you've moved away from Him for all the wrong reasons. So, I'll get off my soapbox now, because it's almost time for one of my favorite *I Love Lucy* episodes...the chocolate one! It's the one where she and Ethel get jobs at the chocolate factory and I even got some dipped chocolates for us to enjoy while we watch."

Wow. Sister Mary-Margaret doesn't mince words. I never had these types of conversations with my parents. It was always more about the length of my skirt or bangs.

"I only want to be honest with you. I can't say that I have, without hurt and cynicism, really read the Bible with an open mind. When I lost my family, I just shut down. I wanted my mom and sister to be here, it's all I could think about." I say.

"I will never propose to have an answer for you as to why you have lost your family, but I do know there is a bigger story with a plan and a purpose. I hope you will read the Book of John. Do it with an open heart, willing to be honest with what you find, and honest with yourself. Don't read it thinking about your dad, your family, your religion, or anything else. Just read it with fresh eyes, willing to see what Jesus is saying to you, Piper Penn, right here today in 1979. Now let's have some chocolates and laugh our heads off!" she says.

There's that cleansing giggle.

Turning up the TV as the credits roll, she excuses herself to go in the kitchen and get the chocolates for us. I feel something, a tear in my heart, a crumbling, a vulnerability. I feel—could it be hope? And, this time, I know I will look at my new Bible with different eyes, not as an assignment, but more like a lifeline thrown my way.

* * *

Riding back to the Grand, all I can think of is how sure of myself I have been the last few years. Or confused. I just wanted to be left alone. I even thought of ending it all—just leaving it all behind. It was mostly stupid Freddy and his weekly coffee visits that stopped me. I didn't want to mess with his head. It was always just after I had seen him, or a few days until I was going to see him again, and the timing never seemed right. Honestly, without those weekly meetings, I just might have done it.

Freddy writes me every week. Shaky, scribbly letters about how late the mail carrier is or how he doesn't like the sub-lessee he found. He says he's a hippie, probably because he has long hair, but that he couldn't be choosy if I was going to get my rent paid. I keep sending him a postcard of Mackinac Island every week, and mostly I just keep the correspondence light. I don't want to tell him much and get him revved up. A revved-up Freddy is not a pretty sight. At least he now has accepted that I won't be back until the three months are up, and coming back at all is up in the air. Part of me thinks I'm crazy to stay here. It often feels like I'm in a different country altogether, it's so foreign to what I know in San Francisco. But, I'm never quite sure if that is a good or bad thing. There's really nothing for me there anymore except Freddy and easy access to movies. I do miss the quirky people that live there, like Frap. Here, there's a commonality among the locals, mostly because they are all related and have very similar backgrounds. Comforting and scary all at the same time, especially when it comes to

Katherine. What was that note she referred to, and why did it set her off so much?

That's it. I'm not from here, I am from San Francisco. We don't sit around and wonder about things; we get in your face and ask you. Cam let me know as he rushed by one day that he doesn't have any news, and it seems, he will keep avoiding Katherine. Maybe I just need to be more direct. People here insinuate and walk around subjects and cloak their real meanings so they can never get called on the carpet for rudeness. No more. Tomorrow I'm going to Katherine's office. She said to stop by anytime, so I will. I'm going to directly ask her what she meant by a note passing under her door. It's time for some truth about these island people!

Chapter Fourteen

Walking to Katherine's office downtown, I keep giving myself pep talks, so I don't chicken out. This feels right and even righteous in some way. Entering the building, I see her name two doors down. There's a buzzer to press. Here goes nothing.

"Yes, may I help you?" the voice on the other side of the wall says.

"Hello, yes, Miss Penn here to see Mrs. Sims-Dubois if she is available."

"Miss Penn, well of course, I'll open the door for you momentarily." It is Katherine answering her own buzzer, but I think she's trying to act as if she had a secretary. She has a welcoming look as she ushers me into her small but luxuriously decorated office. Her desk looks fit for a queen with scrolling woodwork around the edges. Ironic. I'm not sure who did the paintings on the wall, but they're not my taste. Maybe they are from a famous artist, but with the abstract look, I don't know who! And the velvet drapes! That goes well with the fluffy carpeting.

"What a lovely surprise. I was hoping we would meet again soon under better circumstances than that rather unpleasant little incident from the other day. I rather lost my bearings, and, that's just not something I do. I'm normally more aware of the importance of composure and social graces and I usually live up to my own high standards. Frankly, I'm quite embarrassed, and I hope you won't hold it against me," she says.

"Well, I thought seeing you in person would be a good idea, to help clear the air," I say.

"Indeed. And, have they caught the thief who stole the jewelry?"

"Honestly, I don't know. We haven't had a meeting since the one you were at, and I think they want to keep things quiet as much as possible and be about the business of making the movie. Katherine, I don't want to get in the middle of a family matter, but I did ask Cam about something you mentioned, and he knows nothing about it."

"Oh?" She seems to bristle a little more.

"You said something about a note put under your door, and it seemed like you thought he put the note there. From what he said, and I believe him, he doesn't know anything about a note. What note did you get—is someone trying to hurt you?" I ask.

"I'm not sure if we know each other well enough for me to divulge that information. I've considered going to the police because it was very unnerving to get that type of note. It was one of those where each letter is cut out from a magazine, so it's not handwritten. It said something very hurtful about my standing in the community, and it was, in my opinion, a sort of blackmail, promising to divulge untrue information if I didn't keep my nose out of other people's business. There was no request for anything other than that. But the information was of a sensitive nature, and only those in our family would have this information. It's not common knowledge what was said, and I thought perhaps Cam did it because he possibly would know certain things, things he might have heard from his parents. These things that are no one's business but mine. I can't think of anyone else who could have sent the note, and the purpose seemed just to be hateful and hurt me. So, I wanted to assure him that I wasn't going to take it, and he better not be threatening me."

"Wouldn't it have been easier to just ask him in private if he sent the note?"

"Well, he won't talk to me, and frankly, I didn't intend to accuse him right then, it just sort of happened in the moment. So, you said he was a colleague and not your boyfriend, but I do detect that you fancy him. Am I wrong?"

"As you mentioned, there aren't a lot of non-tourist people, and since I'm here getting things taken care of, it has been fun to get to know him—having a friendship with someone my own age."

"Yes, and you wouldn't want there to be gossip, I mean since he has a serious girlfriend and all."

Wait, what? I feel my face flushing. I will not let on to this venomous woman that Cam has never mentioned a girlfriend!

"Or, perhaps you don't you know about Vivian? She's the niece of the hotel owner, as I'm sure he told you. She's been off to Europe, seeing the sights. Such wealth and opportunity. Cam's people are very into seizing opportunities when they present themselves," she says.

I hope she's not catching on; I'm trying to keep a poker face.

"As I mentioned, we are friends," I say.

I've got to change the subject. I can't let on I didn't know a thing about Vivian or how stupid I feel that Cam has never mentioned her. Unfortunately, my poker face plan feels like it's failing miserably. My teeth are grinding, and I think my cheek might be visibly twitching! Still, I've got to take back control of this conversation.

"So, if Cam didn't put this note under your door, aren't you concerned that someone is causing trouble and that you should rethink your decision about taking it to the police?" I ask.

"It's always an option, but I will decide if I need to. And, as I said, there was nothing asked for or bodily harm alluded to, so I'm not sure the police would take it seriously. It's just a hurtful thing to me personally.

I have a place in this town unlike any other, and I don't like to see that trifled with for any reason. I just hope the Cam I know, and the Cam you think you know are the same person. Perhaps when Vivian gets back soon, you can see what you think of their relationship. I've always thought he's a gold digger and dating her for her money. Then of course, your inheritance can be considerable, especially if you sell your property, so maybe you should be watching your back too. I do hope you are seriously considering selling your property. We are all from here, and know our world, but it must be very odd for someone like you from the big city. Perhaps we are just too different for you to be truly happy here. And, I'm sure, you could have a very nice life in a place you are used to if you choose to sell. When might you be making that decision?" she asks.

I'm glad I've never told her about the stipulation to live here for three months to get the inheritance. The less she knows, the better. I don't want her to have any deadlines to cause more trouble for me. This way she must at least try to be decent to me to get me to sell. I still wonder if she was the person listening in the woods, but then I don't think she could outrun Cam, especially in her signature high heels.

"I really don't know. I'm taking one day at a time. Have you ever been to San Francisco?" I ask.

"Oh no, no. I've stayed close to my land and my people. This is where I belong. I have no desire to see faraway places—my short stint in boarding school in England taught me that. Everything I have and need is right here on our little island. And, as you know, I will let nothing, and no one, disturb our little piece of paradise," she says. "I'm always making sure things are just as they should be, you can be sure of that."

"Do you ever go to the labyrinth below the Grand Hotel?" I ask.

"What an odd question," she says.

I'm trying to watch her demeanor to see if she is lying, but with her, who can tell.

"I don't frequent labra, labora...whatever you're talking about, it's not for me," she says.

That does seem a sincere response, unless she's that good at lying.

"Well, I've taken up enough of your time, Katherine. Thanks for seeing me. Maybe the note was just a prank or something and will amount to nothing. And, I do hope you and Cam can mend your division at some point," I say, standing up and heading for the door. I'm ready to get out of here.

"You're young, Miss Penn. You might be much happier settling down with the people you know. And another word of advice? Tread lightly around the redhead. Things aren't always as they seem. My sources tell me that there's a proposal awaiting her when she gets back complete with a diamond ring of some magnitude. As far as I know, groundskeepers don't make that much money, even at the Grand Hotel. And you know what they say, all's fair in love and war."

Now I feel her almost pushing me out the door.

"You have to wonder how he got the money for that big diamond ring for her. Well, you run along, and have a lovely day, Miss Penn. Tah!" Katherine says with a real push this time, as she quickly shuts the door behind me.

An engagement? A girlfriend? Why is this the first I'm hearing about someone named Vivian? And why do I suddenly want to slap the redhead even more than I want to slap Katherine?

Chapter Fifteen

It's probably a good thing that I'm walking back up to the Grand. I feel like my head is going to explode and I need to move fast to burn off some anger. Am I just an idiot? Has this guy been playing me all along to see if I will get an inheritance that he can home in on, or is he waiting to see which girl in his life will bring the best monetary gain? Are all men users? I'm starting to wonder. Is Cam closer to the picture Katherine paints? After all, she knows his background and his family. I've known him a very short amount of time, and I haven't been thinking clearly the last few years. But, the night in the labyrinth. It breaks my heart to think that it might have been an act.

I'm due on set today, and Cam and I are in the same scene. We're both working in the background while Christopher Reeve checks into the hotel. There's always a lot of time between take setups, and originally, I was excited to get this extra time to hang out with Cam, but now I don't know how to act. Or, maybe I will really have to "act" to not turn our upcoming conversation into a real scene in front of everyone. I don't want to be like Katherine; hopefully I have a little more sensitivity than that. So, all right. I'm going to say a prayer. I'm trying to open my mind in the way that Mary-Margaret asked me to.

Dear Lord, Help.

There. Short and to the point. And that's all I have time for right now. Quickly running up to my room, I change into my maid costume before making my way to the set in the parlor and signing in for today's shoot.

"All right, guys and gals, quiet down." The director is getting ready to do his thing.

"In this scene, Christopher's character is checking into the hotel, so we are getting the background B-roll shots that we will cut away to when the camera is not on him at the counter. Basically, you will be doing your daily work—sweeping, dusting, tidying. Look busy but not out of place. Don't make any grand hand gestures or call attention to yourself, please. Let's have you move over to the left near her, closer."

He's gesturing for Cam to come closer to me.

"You both work in that area, fussing over the furniture," the director says.

I haven't made eye contact with Cam yet, but I feel like he's staring at me.

"And action!"

Cam and I both work on moving a few pillows around as I begin to dust a lamp, staring only at what I'm doing.

"Cut, okay, let me take a look at that, hold on everyone," the director says.

"Piper, how are you? I've missed you. We had a tulip emergency so I couldn't stop by. How's it going?" Cam whispers, being careful to stay in place for the next shot.

"All right, looking good, let's go again," the director says. "And, action!"

I move again, dusting, and Cam moves closer as we both hit the same pillow at the exact same time. His hand brushes mine and I feel my cheeks flush.

"Keep moving, people, keep tidying… good, and cut! That's good, I think we have what we need. Let's set up the next shot. All right, this set of extras is excused. Check your schedule for your next date."

"Cam, I need to talk to…" before I can finish my sentence, a woman yells his name from across the parlor.

"Cam! Cam! I'm back, I'm home, and I've missed you, darling!"

Don't tell me. Vivian, I presume. Cam looks at me with his eyes popped wide open as she moves toward us.

"We need to talk, and I mean really talk, but please, Piper, don't jump to conclusions before we do. Will you promise me that?" Cam says in a low whisper.

Before I can answer, Vivian has grabbed his arm and plants a big kiss on him. Cam looks at me like the fox in the hen house, and it's his turn to turn redder than his hair.

"My Cammy Wuzzy Woo, how I've missed you! And you naughty boy, you didn't write half as much as you said you would. Wait, when did we get old-fashioned maids here?" Vivian says looking at me.

"This is part of the movie being made here, Vivian, this is my friend Piper, she's one of the extras on the movie, just like I am," Cam says.

"Oh good, I was going to mention that your wardrobe needs updating! Hello, Pam." Vivian puts her gloved hand forward for me to shake.

"No, it's Piper," I say with a barely-there handshake. "Nice to meet you. Well, I have places to be. See yah."

"Piper, wait…" Cam says.

"Can't, have to be places, toodle-ooh," I say hurrying away.

Again, with the toodle-ooh? The stupid things I say when I'm nervous. So that's the Vivian that is the love of Cam's life. Well, interesting choice. She doesn't come off as the brightest light bulb, but then who am I to say? Besides, she's rich. Beauty will obviously get her much further in life. And, she is quite beautiful. What cute kids they will have. His red hair and her big eyes. Perfect. The perfect couple. I hope they live happily ever after because I won't be around here long enough to find out. I'll finish up the store, sell it, and get the heck out of here and back where I belong. It seems I must have left my heart in San Fran all along. This beautiful, deceptive island isn't paradise for me after all. It's inhabited by a bunch of liars and hypocrites. Except for Sister Mary-Margaret. That's probably because she's not from here.

"Miss Penn, wait up!" Almost to my room, Marcel, my favorite porter, catches up with me.

"Mr. Cam caught me all panicked and asked me to give you this message. Please meet me, that's what he said. He said you would know where, and please meet him at 3 p.m. He said please make sure to meet him," Marcel says.

"Thanks, Marcel. I got the message. I can take it from here," I say opening my door.

"Very good, milady."

I can't take this. Tears are coming. I have to lie down before I faint. I probably should meet Cam at three just to tell him off. Oh great, in an hour. Part of me just wants to leave him sitting there. That would serve him right. I feel humiliated, confused, and jealous. Yes, I'm jealous. I guess I like him. There. I admit it. I like him. A lot. But, I'm mad at myself for letting myself like him. I should have kept my distance. Maybe a quick cleanup and change of clothes will help me feel better. I'm going to write in my diary to clear my head. And I know just who I'm going to write to. Too bad there's not a Tiffany's on the island.

Dear Audrey Hepburn,

Did you have a good time saying the lines in Breakfast at Tiffany's about rats and super-rats, the rats in rat's clothing? I get it now. I so get it. Guys who appear to be one way and turn out to be another way. I've encountered a possible rat, or a super-rat, I'm not sure. You kept saying no one could own you, but they thought they could. I get that too. I'm wondering how to get back at this super-rat. Or is it even worth my time? Maybe I should just keep

my nose to the grindstone, get my place done, sell it, and get out of town.
Anyway, Audrey, I love your movie. I always have. Now I really get it. I
understand what you were feeling. I know why you just wanted to get on
with your life and leave the guy behind. But you stayed. Please tell me you
stayed for the cat.

A big fan,
Piper

All right, Cam. Time to really show me why you deserve an Academy Award with the acting job you're about to perform. I'm going to be judging your performance as you explain that you never once mentioned you were seeing someone while you were giving me a kiss goodnight.

As I head for the labyrinth, I hope it's empty. Thankfully, very few people go there. At least it's always been private when I've stopped except for the shuffling feet we heard. This isn't the same expectancy I had when I came here before, not a good, relaxing feeling. It's become a favorite reflection spot, and I hope it's not just one more thing Cam is about to ruin for me. Nothing like a cheating man to ruin the sacred.

"Piper. Thank you for at least coming. I know you must be very mad, but please, give me a chance to explain," Cam says pulling me down next to him on the bench near the start of the prayer circle.

I pop back up and jump in front of him.

"I'm not sure I'm staying, Cam. I'm not sure of anything right now when it comes to you. Someone told me that you are about to become engaged to a girl you know very well, a certain Vivian. And that you have a huge diamond to offer her. Thank you for not getting down on one knee in front of me," I say.

"What? Who told you that? I don't have a diamond, and I'm not getting engaged. Yes, I did date Vivian over the past year, but she left for Europe and I made no promises to her, no matter what you heard."

"Well that big juicy kiss made it seem like she thought there was a commitment. And, really? You didn't even mention her to me?"

"That's just the way she is. I didn't initiate it. I haven't been writing to her as you did hear her say because after we met, I totally lost interest in her. Who told you I was getting engaged?"

"Your favorite cousin, of course."

"Katherine? You talked to Katherine about me and my life?"

"I went to see her to find out about the note under her door that she thinks you put there. I went to clear it up and help you."

"I told you I had nothing to do with that note. Why do you believe what she says over what I say?"

"Well, let's be fair. She at least told me you were seeing someone, and that's more than I heard from you! I would have been doubly surprised before if Vivian had showed up with her big kiss. At least I had some idea of what was going on, thanks to Katherine."

"Piper, listen to me. I did date Vivian before, but it was nothing once she left. I should have mentioned it, but it never really seemed right, and to me it was in the past, so I didn't see why I should bring it up. I had no idea when she was coming back. She's in the past. I didn't think you would care about her at all."

"People at the hotel who know you were probably looking at me like I was some sort of goofus who was having coffee with a guy who was already dating a girl they all knew."

"Really? I don't sit and think about what other people think. I don't care what they think, but I do care what you think about me. Very much. I never tried to deceive you, and I am sick that you are hurt. I want to fix it and make it right. I want you to believe me, and I don't want to lose your trust. You mean too much to me," Cam says in a softer tone. "Please sit down here and let's just talk, please."

"All right, I'll sit down, but mostly because my feet hurt," I say.

"Oh, well, I'll take any reason," Cam says.

"Well, I'm sure Vivian is pretty startled too. She seems to be in the frame of mind that you and she are a thing," I say, making sure to sit on the far side of the bench.

"Right after you left, I sat down with her and told her, in no uncertain terms, that we were just friends, and I reminded her that I had told her that when she left too," Cam says.

"Did she accept it?" I ask.

"Yes, she made a remark about all the guys that she can't wait to get back to in Europe, and how she's only here for a few days before she leaves again. And then she said I was never really her type and she hates red hair," Cam says.

I can't help but bust out laughing at that last part because I know he made it up.

"Now, let's get back to the part where you were talking to Katherine about me. Piper, come on! She's not someone you should ever go see or engage in any way. And for being a Miss know-it-all, she was way off on the information about me and Vivian. That just shows you that she dwells in gossip instead of reality. Who even knows if there was a note or if she fabricated it in her head?" Cam asks.

"No, there's a note. She seemed really shook up when she talked about it. She said that it could only have been written by someone who knows her family background and it would threaten her devotion to the family or something like that. It was one of those notes that was cut out letter by letter from a magazine."

"Did she show you the note?"

"No… she doesn't trust me because I know you, and she also wants to stay somewhat in my good graces because she wants me to sell to her. Can you think of something you would know that your parents knew and passed on to you?"

"I really can't. My parents wanted nothing to do with her. Honestly, I think she's crazy. Plus, I'm a guy. We don't pay attention to that kind of stuff."

"Well, at least you admit it!"

"So, can there be forgiveness all around? Me, because I should have mentioned Vivian to you in some capacity, and you, because you obviously don't always have good judgment as evidenced by your visit to Morticia! Now the fact that you did decide to come here and meet me shows good judgment, so I think you are already fixed!"

"Wow, good thing you have a button-down shirt on today, so you can fit it over your head!" I say, socking him in the arm.

Cam pulls me close and hugs me.

"I was sick today when I thought I was losing you. You are very special to me, Piper Penn. Please know that."

"You are very special to me too, but please, no more Vivian surprises. I need to know a man I can trust."

"I get that. You'll see, I'm one of the good guys. I want your trust."

"You're on probation, Mister. We'll see how you do. Just remember, I'm watching you."

All I can think about after closing the door after Cam walked me back to my room is: I hope you don't let me down, Cam. Either you are who you say you are, or I'm going to find out I have no real sense when it comes to knowing people. But I can promise you this, Mr. Red, if you do let me down again, there won't be another chance.

Chapter Sixteen

The weeks are starting to fly by, and life is taking on a new rhythm, which I only realize when I stop to catch my breath because it's *I Love Lucy* day with Sister Mary-Margaret. Each week opens the door for new hilarity and new stories, and with every episode, I feel closer to her because she's so genuine. If anyone would have told me I would have had any interest in talking about the Bible and looking at it more closely while watching *I Love Lucy* with a nun, I would have thought they were eating the brownies. But no matter what I say to her about my life or my thoughts, there's no judgment. There's just the invitation to look at it with fresh eyes. My dad, and even my mom to some extent, dwelt in staying on God's good side. It felt like they were always wondering how the big judges in the sky were going to react to our latest misstep. Mary-Margaret never waters down her belief, or is afraid to question my observations, but I always feel heard, and understood. She told me she's not afraid to question God on anything or be honest with Him. She also said she doesn't think He's afraid of the hard questions, even if we don't believe. From the freezer episode to Lucy doing the TV commercial, to the camping trip, to her ballet class—we laugh, and along the way she teaches me. Last night she stopped cold in the middle of a laugh and looked at me.

"Piper, please forgive me."

"Forgive you, for what?"

"Well, I told you that I wouldn't talk about faith things until you wanted to, and I don't know that you really ever gave me permission. Yet every week, here I am, bringing up Jesus, Joseph, Mary, Jonah, Abraham, Paul, Peter... everyone! I feel like I wasn't true to what I promised you."

"Well, I never changed the subject, did I? I think you know me well enough by now that if I really didn't want a subject to continue in our conversation, I would have veered away or shut it down. I guess, my permission was unspoken. Besides, I've never seen things the way you talk about them, and I love the way you enjoy the Bible, Jesus, and God. I get why you love your faith. I'm making my way back, and I don't want to lose it again."

"Remember the verse you know from your childhood, John 3:16? Remember how it starts?" Sister asks.

"God so loved the world..."

"Yes. So instead of 'the world,' let's put your name in there. God so loved Piper that He sent His Son, and if Piper believes in Him, she won't perish, but will have everlasting life. There's nothing especially spiritual about being a nun. In the Lord's eyes, I'm just another one of His children that He loves, and this is the journey He has for me. It's no more important than anyone else's journey. Obviously, you've been given a talent as an artist. I simply adore the picture you painted, by the way. I'll cherish it forever. Piper, you have a great sense of humor, and you recognize great comedy when you see it. I've never had kids, of course, but I can imagine that as a parent, you love each one for who they are. And when you have multiple children, you don't run out of love. I think God is that way. He's just crazy about each of us. All we have to do is accept that and love Him back in the way He's asked us to in his love letter to us. Then He's just there as the best dad that ever was to guide us, advise us, and love us."

"For God loved Piper... that kind of blows me away..." I say quietly.

"It's been my experience that He speaks to us in multiple ways. Some people think because they don't hear an audible voice, God isn't speaking, but that's not true. He does talk to us through the Bible, other people He brings into our lives, and everything that He's given us in this life. Even the beauty of this island speaks of Him in different ways to different people. It's all quite magnificent, isn't it?" she says softly.

"Only God could have thought up this place. It's one-of-a-kind, that's for sure," I say.

"It really is. I never tire of seeing it new every morning. Have you finished reading all of John yet?"

"In sort of a skimming way, but I'm going back through it more slowly, to really soak it in. I hear your voice over my shoulder when I read, encouraging me to really see the story that's happening."

"Ha, me on your shoulder, I love that. You know one of my favorite Bible verses is in John, and I don't think it's one that's quoted a lot, but I think it really is one of the very best verses if there can be such a thing. It's John 21:25, and as I remember it, and don't mind if I paraphrase a bit, it says that Jesus did many other things beyond what we read in the Bible. And here's the part that just gets me. It says that if every one of them were written down, there would probably not be enough room in the whole world for the books that would have to be written to contain it all."

"See, now that didn't pop out at me yet, but yes, that is pretty astounding."

"I like to think that He feels that way about each one of us. If we ever understood all the ways He thinks about us, and loves us, and provides for us, and protects us, and laughs with us, and plays with us... well... there wouldn't be enough paper in the whole world to hold down everything that could be written."

"Wow, now you made me cry again. Pass the tissues, please."

"Oh, remember in *Gone with the Wind* when Rhett says to Scarlett, that he's never known her to have a hanky in any life crisis? Ha, that's you, Piper! Here's your tissue."

"Don't mind me. Keep going."

"We talk about the major Bible people beyond Jesus like Paul and Peter but think about all the people mentioned in the Bible who only have their names and not their story. We don't know their stories beyond a mention, yet God wanted them in there. That just speaks to the importance of every single person. It's become a special study for me, to seek out these minor characters, to give some thought to them too. Remember when I told you I love Ethel? Here's why Ethel, and all the Ethels that ever lived are so important! Very few of us will be the stars, the Lucys of the world, as it were. If that is our focus, then we miss out on how important it is to be who we're made to be and what we have each individually been called to accomplish. There's something unique for each person God made, something only they can do that He has called them to, if they will listen. Our focus on being only Lucy or being unhappy can keep us from what we should be focusing on—ourselves—the Ethel that we probably are. Think about who we focus on in the Bible, I don't mean God or Jesus of course, but the people we learn about. Who did you learn about?"

"Let's see. Matthew, Mark, Luke, John, Paul, Peter, Noah, Jonah… like that. Oh, Adam and Moses too. Mostly in flannelgraph lessons."

"Flannelgraph?"

"Yes, the teacher has a board and she put flannel characters up on the board and tells the Bible stories. That's where I got most of my education."

"Oh, got it. Yes, now that you mention it, I think I was in on a few of those type of lessons too. So, we know these types of people, the famous ones…the Lucys of their time, you might say."

"Good one, I get that!"

"But think about this. Every person He chose to be mentioned or referred to in some way were just as important to Him. Do you know the names Elishama, Ehud, Jabez, Shiphrah or Puah?"

"Shama, Jaba, Papa, who??? No! I grew up with many stories, but I have never heard those. They're in the Bible? They don't make it into the sermons throughout the year, I'll tell you that."

"Elishama is in the Book of Jeremiah, chapter 36, verse 21, a guy who is a scribe, or court secretary as we might call him today. A seemingly insignificant mention of a name to us, but not to God, He put it in His word, the Bible. A person with a name, a family, a life, thoughts, and feelings, just like you and me."

"Real people. More than cardboard characters. I never gave much thought to any of the Bible people I learned about growing up as flesh and blood, really. They seemed so one-dimensional. I never think about them living real lives, or really living at all, I guess. They seem like stories that didn't actually happen."

"I agree, that's how we look at them, and when we do, we lose the very human experience that Jesus had too. As you are reading in John, look closely at how Jesus became flesh and came to see us, starting as that baby who we also turn into a cardboard character at Christmas. When we don't really think of Him, or God, or Mary in terms of reality, they become stories that are easy to discard, and we miss out on so much!"

"What happened with the other names you mentioned?"

"Ehud in Judges 3, a guy with a big sword who assassinated a king and liberated God's people. Jabez from first Chronicles who says an amazing prayer and shows us God listens and wants to bless us."

"How do you remember all of this? And the other names cracked me up…Shiplah?"

"Ha, no, it's Shiphrah and Puah, pretty obscurely mentioned, but they did something amazing! They were midwives who defied the king and were ordered to kill the Hebrew baby boys—it's in the book of Exodus. They came up with a tale to save the babies, and still not get in trouble at the same time. When you're done with John, you must find these stories. I'll write them down before you leave, where to find them, so you can look them up. But first you have to finish the Book of John!"

"Yes, ma'am, you are giving me enough homework to keep me very busy. Oh, sorry for calling you ma'am—I hate that!"

"Ha! No ma'ams for us young gals. But, Piper, I hope you see the truth I really want to share with you. Don't be afraid of being who you were called to be, whether it's Lucy or Ethel, both equally important to the story. We are all extremely important to God's great story of mankind. All those names in the Bible are there to teach us more about who God is and who we are to Him. Missing that lesson in life would be a tragedy. And, I hope right about now, you don't think I invite you here every week simply to preach at you! It's just that, I don't know... there's something there. I have known you a very short time, but I feel like I really get you, and you get me. That's something special and it doesn't happen that often in life, so I don't want to take it for granted or let it pass me by. Now I've probably gone overboard—I do that—and I wouldn't blame you if you run out of here, Lucy or no Lucy!"

"No, not at all. I totally get what you're saying. I feel closer to you than people I've known for many years, and I also get that it's hard to put into words that match up to what it is, and I'm okay with that. You don't frighten me, you encourage me, and I'll take all of that I can get. You also know a lot of my story, but I feel like maybe you're getting the bright shiny side, and there's a dark underbelly that you wouldn't like or approve of."

"Oh, so you're human, and you want me to judge you for that? Sorry. No can do. Please don't think I'm all bright and shiny either. Don't let this habit fool you. Yes, things improved on the outside when I became a nun, but I know God is looking in the heart, and I can go down a dark alley just like anyone else. But I don't think that's our heart's desires. I think we both want more of what God has for us, and that is our spark when we meet. He's taking the joy of a '50s sitcom and the fun of movies and bringing us together to seek out that better way. Maybe as each other's encourager, we can get there with fewer bumps along the way. I remember the words I couldn't think of. We are kindred spirits."

"Kindred spirits. Okay, now you've got the tears flowing again. How you accept me, not judge me, it's not something I'm used to. And, when I see it, or sense it, I want to crumble. It touches something deep in me. It touches a wall I know I've built with anger, brick by brick. You're helping me see things so differently. I get what you're trying to tell me. I only hope I can believe it's true for me. I can see it for everyone else, but not have it apply to me, that God feels that way about me, too. But I'm willing to see what happens."

"A father in the Bible told Jesus that he believed, but he needs help with his unbelief. That's an honest, solid prayer, one I pray often. I think if you tell the Lord that you do believe, but you want help with your unbelief, that you will be astounded on how that prayer will be answered."

"Yes, you've stirred my memory on that story. I had forgotten it. Help my unbelief. That is a good prayer for me to remember."

"Well, my dear, shall we watch our crazy friends Lucy and Ethel and see what shenanigans they are up to this week?"

"I can't believe how fast time goes when we start talking. I thought we would have so much time, but here the show is about to start. Oh, I know this one! They're trying to get a car to drive to California… it's a good one!"

"Here's your soda, here's the popcorn, and let's get ready for some fun!"

And then, she starts to giggle. Dear Lord, thank you for bringing me to Sister Mary-Margaret. It's like you gave me back a little bit of my mother in a way that I could handle and not turn away. The half-hour flies by as Lucy and Ethel manage to get in and out of trouble and end the episode with the same zest for life that they show up with each week.

"That was a good one. I love their clothes, and the car... pretty cool," I say. "Sister, there's something that just doesn't quite add up for me, not with Lucy and Ethel, but back to the other things we've been talking about."

"Hey, no holds barred here, ask away."

"You know so much about the Bible, and you're a nun, but you don't tell me I have to follow your exact path. I've never experienced that when I'm with religious people. Usually there's a push to their doctrine or way of viewing God with rules. I don't get that from you. What is your story?"

"I guess my background is a little different than a lot of nuns. I was abandoned by my mother at birth. You might think she would leave me at a nunnery, fairly common at that time, but she left me at the entrance of a fire station. The fire chief called his brother and sister-in-law to come and get me. Things were less formal back then in the small town where I was raised. My father was a Catholic, and my mother was a Protestant. So, I was both. I went to a Catholic church with my father on Saturdays and to the Protestant Church with my Mother on Sundays. I did the kid and youth programs at both churches. I grew up spending a lot of my time in church, and through the process, I came to know and love the Bible. But it really all came together when I started exploring it for myself, not waiting on someone else to tell me more. That's probably why I'm just one to talk about God and Jesus first and foremost. It's not calculated in any way, it's just my life. If someone ever has an interest in my faith, I'm happy to answer any questions. It's never been about religion for me, much more about a true relationship and being real. I'm a woman of the 1960s, so there's a little rebel in me too. That and the Holy Spirit, and I'll take any chance presented to me to love people and tell them about the Kingdom of God. It's the essence of life and I can't stand the thought of people missing out, and they are missing out if they don't know."

"Did you have a hard time with the fact that you weren't with your birth mom, or did you have a desire to find more about that?"

"I really didn't. I mean, I wonder if I look like her, since obviously I don't look like my parents at all. They were the ones who did the work to raise me and keep God in my life, more than most, to say the least. I can only feel that it all worked out for the good, just as God knew it would."

"Were your parents trying to convince each other that they were the right religion?"

"Another really cool thing. They didn't. They respected each other and would go to each other's church on occasion. They were endearing people who I still miss every day. They both have passed, my mom from breast cancer and my dad just a year later from pancreatic cancer. I was just eighteen. I have no siblings, so I know your feelings of being alone in a sense."

"Oh, Mary-Margaret, I just go on and on about myself, and I don't even think of another person's pain. I'm so sorry. Please forgive me, I feel so stupid!"

"No, I don't feel that way. I have a few years on you, I've had more time to adjust to the changes, and entering the convent gave me a strong family bond through the church that has been a foundation of love for me. Perhaps there's a family foundation for you here on the island. I will pray that you get a sense of what path you should take."

"You're an orphan, I'm an orphan, and Cam, my good friend at the Grand, his parents were killed in a car accident... also an orphan. And we have all met, that blows me away."

"And yet, when we are adopted into God's family, we aren't orphans, because we are His children in the best forever family we could ever imagine. And think about this, God brought us into each other's lives knowing we could comfort each other. We all really understand how hard it is to lose your parents, and you, your sister too. No coincidences, Piper."

"I'm seeing it. No coincidences," I say.

"I see your face when you speak about Cam. Could it be that you are feeling something beyond friendship? I don't know him at all, but I think I have seen him from a distance once or twice. Are you sure he's not related to Lucy? That red hair! Okay, the color of your face blushing right now speaks volumes!"

"Well, since they won't let cast talk to Christopher Reeve much, I do have a certain fondness for the redhead. And, speaking of redheads, let's talk about those red curls that peek out from your habit!"

"Ha! Caught! I'm a redhead from way back. Most people don't know these days because I try to cover up all my hair, but it does have a mind of its own, and those darn curls sneak out."

"You know that makes you Lucy and me…"

"That makes you just who you should be, Piper. My friend. Boy, we've covered a lot of topics tonight, and you better catch a taxi before they shut down for the evening."

"You're right, I didn't set up a time, so I'll put in the call right now. They should be here in a jiffy." I do just that, using her phone and wanting to talk more before the taxi arrives.

"You're doing a lot of thinking and coming to grips with a lot of things you've been through, but I feel like I know you, Piper. You're going to have your eyes opened. You're going to see why you are here, and what your call is, just like I did. And, no, I'm not trying to recruit you into being a nun!"

"So, here's a really deep theological question for you."

"Okay, I hope I'm ready for it... shoot."

"What's your all-time favorite *I Love Lucy* episode?"

"Oh my gosh, Piper, that is definitely the hardest question you have ever asked me! Hmm... you know what, I'm gonna have to think on that one and get back to you, because I must figure out which one, and then I must figure out why I picked that one over all the others. Payback time huh? I've given you some things to think about, and now you've given me a doozy! Oh no, there's the buzzer, your taxi is here! Our time together always goes by way too fast. You have a good week ahead. I'll be praying for you. Same bat time, same bat station, as they say on TV! And, Piper, when you lay your head on your pillow tonight and say your prayers, will you be honest with the Father, Son, and Holy Spirit, and let the love and comfort we all so desperately need become your everyday reality forever? That is my honest desire for you."

After my evening with Mary-Margaret I always have a slight headache on the way back up to the Grand. Between the laughing, crying, thinking, and the way I physically feel my heart pound in my body from the things she says to me, I should remember to bring an aspirin with me. It's an overwhelming rush of emotions that I haven't dealt with in quite a few years. Sometimes, I'm not sure I'm the same girl I was before I came to the island this time; I feel like someone totally different. It reminds me of how the house smells when you gather up all the garbage and get rid of it and do a good cleaning. Mary-Margaret is the real deal, but sometimes I still wonder if I am. How could I know so many basics, and still not have it affect the choices I made? But when she was talking about the people in the Bible who aren't the main characters, I thought about the thief on the cross, the one who asked Jesus to remember him when Jesus comes into His Kingdom. He forgave the thief. A thief myself, that hits me. Lord, I am sorry, this time with no justification as to why it was okay. Reaching for another tissue in my jacket pocket, I feel something else, like cloth. It's a hanky with the initials *MM* embroidered on the edge. She just keeps taking care of me in so many ways. But here's a question I can't stop thinking about. I am forgiven, but I have no desire to forgive my father. That might be a thought that's too tough for even Mary-Margaret. I will never forgive my father; he doesn't deserve it.

Chapter Seventeen

"Where's everyone going?" I ask one of the many people rushing downtown past me. I'm heading downtown on my bike, and this is way too many people for this time of day.

"There's a big fire on the corner of Market and Main Street!" a man says hurrying past me.

My place? That's my place! What? I hope the guy is wrong. I also hope I don't knock off one of these people riding my bike like this. No one wants to see a fire happen, but I really don't want my place to be on fire. I'm sure it can't be *The Towering Inferno* with Steve McQueen and Paul Newman, but with all this hubbub it must be bad. Ugh. The smoke smell hits me way before I'm near the corner. Coughing like crazy I whip my bike down. Oh great, a police barricade. At least these firemen are on top of things. Thank goodness there's a fire hydrant close by. Water spray hits me in the face as I get closer to the building. Pushing my way to the front of the crowd, I get within earshot of the police officer.

"Hey, officer, this is my place, can you tell me what's happening?" I ask.

Grabbing my arm, he pulls me around the barricade and yells over the crowd.

"It's your place? Were you just in there?" he asks.

"No, I haven't been here today. It was being remodeled, so I wasn't living here yet," I say.

"All I know so far is there have been multiple witnesses that saw a guy with a hoodie sweatshirt and red hair running out of the building before there was a small explosion and the fire burst out," he says.

"Is the guy with red hair okay?" I ask.

"Why, do you know who it was? We're thinking this is the guy who set the fire and then took off, but he's nowhere to be found."

"I know someone helping me with the remodel who has red hair. His name is Cam Nelson and he works at the Grand, but he wouldn't have set off a fire. He's my friend and helping me." I inwardly cringe as I realize I just implicated Cam. Not good.

"Yah, I know who Cam is. You think he was in there?"

"I'm not sure where he was at today. Joel and Ben Conrad have been working on the building, but they are out of town today. Was anyone hurt?"

"It appears that no one was in the building once the red-haired guy, maybe Cam... ran out... what did you say your name was?"

"Piper Penn, I inherited this place from the former owner."

"Well, we definitely have some questions for this redhead, if it was Cam... he was the last one there. The fact that he was running out right before the fire started seems suspicious. It looks like they're starting to get this under control—they did catch it early—but there's so much smoke. Listen, the best thing you can do now is to make your way to the police station. We have some questions for you. You'll also want to call your insurance person, and I hope you have good insurance. Even though the fire was relatively small, the smoke damage looks quite extensive," he says.

We both start choking, standing so near the smoke. Cam, are you

118

kidding me? Cam has a key because of the remodel, but he would never start a fire on purpose. Maybe a gas valve exploded as he was leaving, but then why would he run away? Why wouldn't he stay here and try to help? There must be a logical explanation for this. He wouldn't purposefully try to sabotage the remodel. But what if this family feud is all a ruse, and he's been working with Katherine to force me out? They wouldn't be the first sneaky people on the planet.

Is it possible this is all a big setup? Maybe I've been an idiot and wandered right into their trap. Did I just walk into a well-thought-through scam like a naïve schoolgirl? I don't even know if I have fire insurance. Heck, I don't know about that kind of stuff at all. I can't stop staring at the building, my building, which is now a mess. I've done it again, been the patsy, the idiot. This family wanted this property and they found a way to get it from me. Are they all working together? Maybe this was all set up even before I came, kind of island con people who always get what they want.

Am I losing my mind?

"All right everyone, it looks like things are under control, so why doesn't everyone just head back to what you were doing?" The policeman is bright red from coughing and yelling. It's no small task to get people to quit gawking and move on.

"Uh, you should get going, Miss Penn, there's nothing you can do here." The officer motions me to be on my way.

I can't believe this. Really, buddy? There's nothing I can do? How about a little revenge on these stupid people? You all think I'm helpless?

The half-block walk to the police station feels like a dream, like the whole world is swirling in smoke and people's faces are distorted with smirks and ridicule. Maybe I'm really seeing them for who they are for the first time. I guess I could try to call Cam and see if he's at the Grand right now. If he can clear it up, I should hold back on this madness I'm feeling. Or maybe he's like the men I've met in my life who use women to get what they want. I don't know what to think. I'm baffled and stunned. I thought he was different.

If there's no insurance I will have lost everything, again. I don't even have enough money for a plane ticket back to San Francisco, and my apartment is sublet. I don't have anywhere to go. God, do you see this? I'm not waiting until I get to the police station. I'm using this phone booth right here, to get answers. Cam can tell me right now. Mom comes through again with her great advice to always have phone money; this dime will do its job. Good, Dinah's voice on the switchboard, at least I know she'll make a good effort to find him. It pays to talk to people at coffee shops.

"Hi, Dinah, this is Piper Penn, and this is kind of an emergency. Is Cam on the premises? I need to speak with him."

"I'm sorry, Cam is out all day on the other side of the island inspecting some of the composting areas for the hotel. He's been gone since early this morning," Dinah says.

"That's right, he did mention something like that. Can you get a message to him somehow?" I ask.

"I can leave a message that you called, Piper, and give it to him when he gets back. He's usually good about checking for messages when he takes a trip. It's kind of sparse over there, so I don't have a way to get him a message," Dinah says.

"Did he go with a crew?" I ask.

"No, I don't think so. They've all been here all day weeding. He does those inspections by himself, usually. He might not be back till after dark, but I will leave a message for him to contact you. Will you be in your room, Piper?" she asks.

"I'm not sure, but yes, if he can try to find me, that would be greatly appreciated. Thanks, Dinah."

I think he did mention something about going on this inspection. Cam, you don't even have a witness to say where you were today. I

120

hope you can prove your alibi. Get back on track, Piper. One of the witnesses at the police station should have more information. My place might be ruined with smoke damage, but what hurts more is realizing Cam could have been planning this the whole time. First, he doesn't mention that he has a "sort of" girlfriend, and now this. Well watch out, buddy. You think redheads have tempers? Wait until you see what I'm capable of!

Chapter Eighteen

Why am I walking to the police station when I brought my bike with me… just shows how rattled I am. Hopefully no one will take my bike. Just a short while ago I would have said that, no, not in this town. People are good, honest, and trustworthy. Well, I guess I need to wake up and grow up. Turns out people burn down buildings to get rid of you while they pretend to be your friend. I can't get over the fact that witnesses saw a redhead coming out of the building. Maybe the people who saw the man running out can clear up this horrible mess.

"Hi, I'm Piper Penn, owner of the building that burned, and I was instructed to come here and make a statement."

"Yes, Miss Penn, please have a seat, we are just finishing up with one of the witnesses." An officer points me toward a chair.

A door opens from a room that looks like something of an interrogation area I've seen on TV shows, and an officer is saying goodbye to Miss Fields!

"Miss Fields! Did you see what happened to my building? Did you see Cam coming out of the building?" I ask.

I know she knows who Cam is. With all her trips to the Grand, she has come across him. I even think I saw her flirting with him a time or two.

"Miss Penn! I'm so sorry about your building, it's just awful! And I'm shocked at what I saw as I was walking past the building, on my way back from the Grand actually—I had to drop off papers again. It was a man in a hooded sweatshirt, and he had that flaming red hair. I hate to say it, but we all know who has that hair in this town. There's no one else with hair that color. I was across the street at a bit of a distance, but sure as shooting, I believe that's who I saw! I'm sorry, but I can't lie, I have to tell what I witnessed," Miss Fields says.

The officer I saw at the scene bursts through the door at that moment and calls to the other officers.

"The questioning will have to wait! The bank was just robbed! All hands on deck. Get to the bank so we can dust for fingerprints and find out everything that was taken!"

With that he runs out the door, with the other officers close behind, grabbing their gear as they go. Only the office secretary and Miss Fields remain. The secretary is staring at me. I don't think she's been put in this position before.

"Um, why don't you fill out your contact info on this form and write down everything you saw once you got to the fire. The officers will have to follow up with you after this current tragedy is over. Man, oh man, what is this world coming to? A fire and now a robbery? That stuff just doesn't happen here! Miss Fields, I think you are free to go, we have your information," the office secretary says.

"What about the other witnesses, did they all see the same thing?" I ask Miss Fields, trying to get her to stop and take my question.

"Yes, it was me and my two girlfriends from high school. They all saw it too, the red-haired man running out of the building right before the smoke billowed out. I don't know Cam very well, but why would he do this?" she asks.

"I am speechless. It's just not like him. Oh, and Miss Fields, do you know from reading all the documents in my inheritance, do I have fire insurance on the building?" I ask.

"Yes, I do remember that was all covered while you had the stipulation of living here for the pre-determined time, so I'm sure you'll be fine. We all want you to be okay, but we need to get the job done," she says.

"Get the job done?" I ask.

"Oh, listen to me not making any sense, get the job done according to the stipulations of the will. Sorry, I've got to get back to the law office. I'm sure it will all be just fine, you'll get the insurance money to rebuild once again, or maybe it will just be easier to sell it. That's always an option, and maybe just head back to your life in San Francisco. The weather is so much better, and you can enjoy the things you love. You could go to a ton of movies," Miss Fields says.

"Yes, wouldn't that be great? I could use a good movie right about now. Well, thanks, Miss Fields. Please be safe. Now with a bank robbery, who knows who you can trust around here? At least we know Cam had nothing to do with that. I'm still so mixed up, anyway, thanks for your help," I say.

Well at least she's nice. I couldn't expect her to lie about what she saw, but the fact that Cam could be involved is making me sick to my stomach. Filling out forms, just what I want to do right now. I'll do the best I can with my mind in a muddle. By the time I get back to the Grand, Cam should be getting back from "inspecting the compost area" if that's what he was really doing. I can't wait to hear his alibi. It better be a good one.

"Here's the completed forms, along with anything I know that might be helpful. I didn't see anything. I got there after the fact, when it was almost over," I say to the office secretary.

"Thanks. You're free to go, and I'm sure an officer will follow up with you, but, please, don't leave the island," she says.

Overstep your bounds much, Miss Receptionist? Geez. Everyone thinks they're Perry Mason. Thankfully, walking back to my property, which is now all soot covered, I find my bike where I left it. Pedaling back, I feel the ache of muscles that refuse to relax. This is all so stressful and everything about it stinks. The guys were more than halfway done with remodeling and now we will have to start over. I hope the money is adequate to pay for the cleanup and rebuild. And, will this all take longer than the time I was given to live at the Grand? Affording a place to live could be a big problem. I'm barely getting by. It takes a pretty penny to live here. This really does mess up everything, including my heart.

Nestling my bike in the secret little place Cam set up for me in the woods by the pool house below the Grand, I lock my bike. It doesn't feel like the serene, secure place it did just a few hours ago. Why would someone who seemed to care so much about me do so much damage and start a fire? Crossing the lawn and heading for the stairs up to the Grand I see Cam heading toward me across the lawn.

"Piper! I just got your message from Dinah! I heard about the fire... and now a robbery? I was cutting my trip short anyway because I forgot some of my supplies. I don't know what's with me lately. Thank goodness, though, because it made me come back earlier. All I could think about is you. Are you okay?" Cam asks reaching to give me a hug.

Forget a hug or anything else, buster!

"Am I okay? Did you get a message from the police yet, because they will be coming to talk to you any minute, I'm sure, as soon as they are done with this robbery stuff."

"Why would they want to talk to me? I was gone on the other side of the island. I don't have anything to add, and in fact, I think the way I smell right now should be pretty good indication that I wasn't around to see anything."

"Oh, so that's how you're going to work the alibi, huh?"

"Alibi? What are you talking about, Piper? Why would I need an alibi? I didn't do anything. I'm guilty of smelling nasty, I'll give you that," Cam says laughing.

"Turn around, Cam. See the police? They're coming to talk to you. See how funny you find that," I say as I turn and head up toward the hotel.

"Piper, what are you talking about?" Cam yells after me.

The officers pass me, and I hear them start to tell Cam they have some questions for him about a certain fire set today on the corner of Market and Main Street. Oh, good acting, Cam! Look and sound surprised! The very thing that I was first attracted to you about is going to be your downfall, mister. Your red hair is going to put you in jail. Maybe I don't know you at all and you've had this coming for a long time. How would I know? Seems I should change my name to Miss Gullible.

"Miss Penn, can you wait up please? I have a few more questions for you too." The officer I saw at the fire is calling me back.

"Yes, I filled out the papers the best I could," I say.

"That's fine for now. In speaking with Miss Fields, I found out you took out additional insurance on your property a month ago. Can you tell me about that?" he asks.

"Additional insurance? I didn't even know if I had insurance at all. This is all part of my inheritance from the former owner. It was all handled in the will. I didn't authorize insurance, or even have a working knowledge about insurance at all. I think you should talk to my lawyer in the firm, Mr. Sawyer. Maybe it's standard procedure or something," I say.

"Well, it seems that the amount of insurance was increased after the initial policy was taken out," he says.

"That's news to me, I don't know anything about the original policy or an increase. But, please, talk to Mr. Sawyer. He should be able to clear any of this up," I say.

"Thanks, I will follow up and get back to you… and one more thing. Do you have any plans to leave the island? I would advise against it until we have wrapped up this investigation," he says.

"I have no plans to leave, but am I in some kind of trouble? Do I need to engage a lawyer to defend me?" I ask.

"I'll be truthful with you, we have done some investigation, and with your past theft record, we just want to make sure you have no plans of leaving suddenly," he says.

Oh great. That makes me look bad when I had nothing to do with this. Now who else is going to be able to find out about my past? Extra insurance? Tom Sawyer better have an answer for this insurance stuff. This is all too much. I need to get back to my room, shut the door on all this mess and take a hot shower. Glancing back, I see Cam going with the officers, probably heading back to the station. I need to sleep. I need this day to be over. I wish, instead of dealing with this, I was sinking into a bubble bath and painting a new picture of Round Island. All I have to do is get through the lobby and make it to my room, my sanctuary.

"Miss Penn!" It's Dinah chasing me down the hall. "You have a telegram!" she says.

"I swear, if I never see another piece of yellow paper again, that would be fine with me," I say.

"Sorry, I'm just the messenger, no need to jump down my throat. I hope it's not bad news."

And with that she hurries on her way. Now, I've gone and been mean to her. Clutching the yellow paper, I just want to get to my room. I don't know if I can stomach one more telegram. And poor Dinah. She must be having some nice thoughts about me right about now. Finally, I can shut my door and see what this blasted piece of paper is about.

No! No, not this! That's it, I can't take it. I let the telegram drop out of my hand and fall on the bed. I can't stop this sobbing because it's coming from the depths of my soul. It doesn't even feel like it's coming from me, but it's making my whole body shake. This time, the telegram is from Freddy.

Dear Pip,

Thought you would want to know. Stop. Mail came from the Bijou that Melvin Goodstar a.k.a. Frap was hit by a car crossing the street and did not survive. Stop. The Bijou contacted all the addresses in his book as a courtesy. Stop. Sorry, Pip, wish I could see you. Stop. Hope you are well. Stop. Fredrick

I can't believe one more person dear to me is gone. Although we weren't related, Frap and I were, what did Mary-Margaret call it, kindred spirits, united by the love of the spark we found in movies. It's such sad news, but I am glad Freddy told me. Frap was one of the good guys, in a world filled with so many bad ones. San Fran isn't the same without good ole Frap. Knowing Frap, he probably had his nose in *Variety* and was reading while crossing the street. I've seen him do it. At any rate, I hope there was no suffering. I hope he had made peace with the Lord, and I wish I had been together enough to talk to him about Heaven. Oh, Frap, you leave me with a good lesson. I so want to go and tell Cam and get a hug. He knew about Frap and how we loved to talk about movies. But now I have no idea if Cam is even someone to trust, or if he's an arsonist. First a liar, now this.

There's a knock at my door.

"Yes?" I ask.

"Piper, it's me," Cam says.

"I'm not sure there's much to say," I manage to say, choking back more sobs.

"Piper, please. Let's talk. Please," Cam says.

Well, if this is going to come to a complete end, I might as well get it over with.

"Come in, the doors open."

He moves toward where I'm on the bed and he looks tired and flushed. "I don't know that I want to see you. Were you able to convince the police of your innocence? Did they buy your alibi even though Miss Fields and her friends clearly saw someone with the type of red hair that only you have running out of my place? Why did you do it? Now there's possibly some extra insurance money taken out on the place that I didn't authorize, but it appears to be done by me. Was this all part of your scheme to have me get a big insurance payoff and then you would scam me out of the money somehow? You're really clever, I have to give you that," I say.

"Piper, stop. Look at me, really look in my face. Is this who you think I am? Really?" Cam asks.

"Hey, buddy. Good con artists are good actors. Maybe I'm a dumb girl from the city sucked into this quaint island fantasy, just ripe for the picking by a good con man. It's not who I want to believe you are, and it's not who I thought you were. But you kept your relationship with Vivian from me. And maybe you're a pro at fooling people. Did I fit perfectly into your plan to get rich? I just can't explain why three people saw you run out of the building," I say.

"Well, first, I was on the other side of the island, and no, I can't prove it because I was alone, other than I do this same project every year on about the same day, so that should show you something. Next, the people who saw what they thought was me can't say for sure it was me. They just saw red hair and assumed it was me."

"Cam! You're the only one with that hair and you know it!"

"There are many tourists who come to the island, so that's a possibility. But, after we're done talking, I'm going to make a phone call. There is someone with hair exactly like mine, only he doesn't live on the island."

"Oh, let me guess, your brother in prison, perhaps?"

"Yes, my brother who I am not close to and for all I know is out of prison. Another possibility. What is making me very suspicious is the fact that the bank was robbed right after the fire. Pretty convenient how the robber was able to get everything done with no attention drawn to himself because of the distraction of the fire. Besides, there was nothing to take in your building, so what was the point? I think the fire was set so the bank could be robbed."

"Did anyone see a redhead coming out of the bank?"

"According to the police, there were no eyewitnesses to the bank robbery because everyone was at the fire. There was only one employee in the bank at the time and she said it was a man with a face mask, so she didn't see any face or hair. It's possible my brother is here and is framing me. The question is why, and who is working with him?"

"Why would your brother not call you when he was getting out?"

"We aren't close, and he's always been jealous of me, saying the baby of the family got all the attention, and had the best from Mom and Dad. If he robbed the bank, he'd have the money he wants, and I would get blamed for it. I'm also wondering if he put the note under Katherine's door to start to stir up trouble and suspicion against me, hoping she would go to the police. I would like to think he wouldn't do something like this, but I really don't know the person he has become in prison. There's still a missing piece, though. Why come here? What's here other than wrecking my life? He could rob a bank anywhere. That's the part I don't get."

He looks down, then up at me again, his expression changing from confusion to sympathy.

"Wait, Piper, why is there a telegram on the floor? Why have you been crying? What happened?" Cam comes and sits next to me on my bed.

"Remember my telling you about my friend Frap who worked at the Bijou in San Francisco? Freddy sent a telegram to say he was hit by a car and died." I can barely get out the last words.

"Oh, Piper, I'm so sorry. You really liked your times with him. It must hurt a lot."

"It hurts immensely," I whisper.

I can't stop my lip from quivering. Everything within me wants to believe this man. I don't know who to believe anymore.

"Piper, I want to be here for you right now. Please believe me. I'm an honest person, I didn't set your place on fire, I didn't rob a bank. Yes, I'm guilty of not being totally honest about Vivian, but that's only because I thought it was over, and there was nothing to tell. I never set out to deceive or hurt you, quite the opposite. From the moment we met, I knew you were special, and that I wanted to get to know you better. Please let me hold you right now. Even if it's just for this moment, let me take some of your hurt. Please let me hold you," Cam says holding out his arms.

I can't stand it. Even if he is a crumb, I need someone right now. Sobbing from the depths of my soul, I lean full-force into his shoulder and let him embrace me. Liar or not, arsonist or not. I feel so alone right now. One more person I'm close to is gone.

Maybe it's me, maybe I caused this in some way? No, I'm not going to go there. That's just stinking thinking as Sister Mary-Margaret would say. Lord, if you're real, give me some wisdom. Give me some hope and show me how to deal with all of this. Show me what to do. I feel as low as I can possibly go.

"Piper, I'm falling in love with you, and I can't bear the thought of you thinking I would ever do anything to hurt you. That's more painful to me than getting accused of crimes I had nothing to do with. Please believe me," Cam whispers gently in my ear as he rubs my back.

"Cam, this isn't the best place to be to be making decisions one way or the other. In my heart of hearts, I do believe you, but why does all this keep happening?"

"I don't know, it all feels like a big test. Maybe as we are both trying to pray to God, the devil is testing us. I mean, that could be a thing, right? He doesn't want us to go that direction, so he is putting things in our path to make us move further away from looking at Jesus. I know that sounds so spiritual and churchy, but maybe everything is meant to be spiritual. I read once that we're not bodies with a spirit, but we're spirits with a body. Maybe we haven't given enough thought and credit to what is really happening in this world."

After a long embrace, we instinctively make our way outside to the bench on my balcony with him holding my hand and leading me to one of our favorite spots. I don't know if I can deny these feelings. I don't think in my heart of hearts he would ever hurt me; I want to know he wouldn't. I love being close to him, how he gently holds my hand, strokes my hair, and looks so deeply into my eyes.

"But, Cam, I feel stupid, naïve. Even though I'm from a big city, I lived a pretty sheltered life growing up, so if you were this person who wanted to fool me, maybe you could. Maybe I would fall for it, and there would be money in it for you. How do I know for sure?" I ask.

"Piper, look at my character. I hope you can see more in me than someone who didn't tell you about Vivian, which again, I thought was over. Can you look at the real me over the time you've known me and say I was capable of that stuff? I can look at the character of my brother, and tell you, he is capable of those things. I'm sorry to say it, but it adds up to how he's lived his life. Also, if you want me to take a lie detector test or something like that, I would do it. I really would. I have nothing to hide. I just can't stand you thinking bad things about me when all I want is for you to think that I have your best interest at heart because of how I feel about you."

"I don't want you to take a lie detector test. I know in my heart you care for me and don't want to hurt me. I believe you. What happens now? What did the police say?"

"Basically, they would feel better if I had an alibi of where I was, but they've been around enough to know people do go work around the island without running into someone. If I drove a car instead of taking a horse and wagon, there would be mileage on the car to show. But, wait, now that we're talking, I did pass this guy that we call 'the hermit' who lives halfway to where I was going. I said 'beautiful day' to him as I drove by with my horses. He didn't acknowledge me, or even seem to look up, but there's a chance he did hear me. If he did, then there it is. I forgot to mention that to the police because it didn't occur to me until just now."

"That would be an alibi, and it couldn't hurt to prove it."

"Okay, I better get that info to the police, and I better make a phone call and see what I can find out about my brother. If he is tied up in all this, there must be more to the story. I swear, Piper, I'm going to get to the bottom of this and show you that I had nothing to do with any of it. Plus, I don't want you feeling scared or unsafe. That's not what this place is about. The lack of fires and robberies is exactly why people live here. We like peace, quiet, and honesty," Cam says, giving my hand a squeeze.

"Do you think Katherine has anything to do with all of this, like she's in some kind of scheme or something?" I ask.

"You know how I feel about the queen, and I would like to say yes, because I would like to go after her, but honestly, no. If my brother is doing something, I think getting her riled up at me was just part of a plan to frame me. But like I said, there's something missing here. Someone here is helping him. I don't think he could pull all of this off on his own," Cam says.

"What if he's still in prison, then what?"

"I'll think about that once I find out for sure, but the first thing is to find out where he is. He could get to the island easy enough with a private boat, or maybe on the commercial ferries. I know those boat guys, so I'm also going to ask if they've seen anyone who looks like me."

"Please keep me posted. I know you're busy, but I would like to know what's going on. This is all very unnerving. I don't even know what's going to happen with the insurance and the rebuilding and if it will all get done in time to meet the deadline before I get kicked out of this place. I love it here, but I have decisions to make and I need to get settled and not feel like a person on a limbo vacation that never knows where they are headed. That's been my life for over four years and it's getting old."

"I will let you know what I find out as soon as I can, I promise. But I don't know where all these questions will take me, even to the point of doing some searching on the island. So, if you don't see me, or hear from me right away, please don't jump to any conclusions. I want this over quickly. I'll also let Dinah know to get you any messages I can get to you right away."

"Oh, she'll be overjoyed to have to track me down. I was pretty rude to her when I got Freddy's telegram."

"Yah, when she told me you were looking for me, she sounded a little snitty. Why don't you drop off one of your cards to her as a gift? I overheard her telling someone how much she loves them but could never afford to get one. That would make her happy. I would like to know I can count on her to help us stay connected through all of this if she can."

"Yes, that's a really good idea. I'll do that first thing in the morning."

"I'm really sorry about Frap, and all of this. We need help beyond ourselves, we need to pray. I'm going to for sure. I know neither of us really know what we're doing, but it's the right direction. And maybe you can talk to your friend Sister Mary-Margaret some more. She could have some insight. Read the Bible for comfort. It's helping me."

"I will. Tomorrow night is our *regular* get-together. I'll have lots to tell her for sure, and she always makes me feel better. She does pray for me. It helps a lot. My whole growing up people said they were praying, and I just always took it for granted, but now it means something. The fact that she's praying means everything right now. I don't know what I'd do without her here, and without..." my voice trails.

Cam moves even closer to me.

"I so hope you're going to say *you don't know what you'd do without me.* I hope that's what you wanted to say. Can I kiss you goodnight, Miss Piper Penn? Would that be all right with you?"

I nod yes, and he pulls me tight and kisses me very tenderly.

"Please know that I am so sorry for the loss of your friend, for everything you are going through. I pray right now that only good things will come out of all of this. I pray we will find who did this, and you will get your place done in the right time frame. Amen," Cam says.

"I think we just prayed together," I whisper.

"And it felt so right, didn't it? Good night, Piper. Angels on your pillow," Cam whispers back.

"Angels on your pillow, Cam," I say. I don't know where he learned that, but I like it.

I close the door behind him. Tomorrow can't come fast enough. We need answers. We need a break. And, why am I suddenly referring to my life as 'we'?

Chapter Nineteen

I know it's a hard time. I know I should be in a puddle on the floor. I should be tossing and turning, unable to sleep. But, that's not what is happening. I feel hope. I feel Cam is telling the truth. And darn it all, I'm going to enjoy another fantastic morning breakfast at the Grand Hotel! Nothing compares to the bacon, the fruit, the egg dishes, the fantastic coffee with cream, the service of the sweet people. This is going to come to an end quite soon, and right now it feels like bacon can fix everything. Usually when life is falling apart, I can't eat. But today, I'm taking a moment to enjoy another lovely croissant with butter and fresh rhubarb jam grown and made right here on the island.

My first stop after breakfast is the switchboard and Dinah. I picked out one of my favorite paintings of Round Island Lighthouse that I hope she'll like. It's tucked in my satchel along with my trusty binoculars and my sketchpad. Okay, big smile as you approach her desk.

"Hi, Dinah!"

"Miss Piper," she replies and turns back to looking at her desk.

Yah, there's a definite chill in the air.

"Listen, Dinah, I want to apologize for how short I was with you about the telegram. I've had so many lately with bad news, but as you said, it's not the messenger's fault, so I wanted to apologize for being short with you," I repeat.

"Don't worry about it," Dinah says. From the expression on her face, I think she feels that she did deserve this apology.

"I also hope that you would accept this small token to show you how sorry I am. I want you to have this card I painted of Round Island Lighthouse," I say giving it to her.

"Oh my gosh, you don't have to do that, but I love it! I love your paintings. I look at them in the gift shop on my break. It's beautiful. Thank you," Dinah says.

"I'm glad you like it, and thanks for all you do with messages for me. I know it's not easy to track me down sometimes, and I do appreciate it so much."

"Well, just doing my job," Dinah says.

The smile on her face as she looks at my picture does make me think she really does like the gesture.

"Oh, that reminds me, there is a note here from Cam! I was going to come and find you..." she says sheepishly.

"Oh, no problem, I took a longer than usual time with a late breakfast this morning, so thanks for this. You have a really good day, and I'm glad you like the painting," I say.

"I love it, thanks," Dinah says with a wave as she answers the switchboard.

Making my way to a white rocking chair on the front porch, I sit down and get ready to read the note from Cam. I'm thankful that he's keeping his promise to keep me up to date the best he can with all the running around he has to do. Seems like eons ago that I first met him on this very porch when he came to greet his visiting friends. I had no idea that the redhead would become so close to my heart. Opening the note, I'm trying not to think much about Frap, but I will do a diary dedication to him for sure. I remember you, Frap, there's just so much to deal with right now. I've also got to do something about Freddy. He's lonely, and my once-a-week coffee dates with him did mean more than I realized. He has no one, and as much as he bugs me, I may be the only someone he has. I can tell by his letters that he misses me and feels lost.

Lord, show me what to do about Freddy. There, I'm saying it. I'm reading the book of John, I'm learning so much more about who Jesus really is, and I'm talking to Him. I don't know if I'm doing it right, or good, but I don't want to fall into a religion trap. I just want to know Him, His Father, and the Holy Spirit. I want to know Them the way Mary-Margaret does. She just loves me and tells me about her relationship with Jesus. And she even finds faith lessons in *I Love Lucy*. After each episode she points out examples of going the extra mile for a friend, faithfulness, and love. And she tells me about more minor people in the Bible that I don't know about, and how they are so important, that everyone is important to Jesus. I'm starting to see that in the book of John.

Why did I miss so much about Jesus while being surrounded by teachings about Him from my parents? Was I too young, or too familiar? That's something I really must explore. But not today. Today, I need to find out what Cam knows, get a few paintings done I promised the gift shop, and head to my evening with Sister Mary-Margaret. She does love movies as much as Frap and I do! She will be sad about Frap; I think she felt like she knew him too as I talked about him and the movies. Maybe someday she can come to San Francisco with me and I can show her the Bijou and where I grew up. Then we can go to LA and put our hands in the handprints of John Wayne at Grauman's Chinese Theatre. I'll have to tell her that tonight; she'll get a big kick out of that. Then she'll let loose with one of her big giggles that happens when we talk about Hollywood or during *I Love Lucy*. She really does love Ethel and their friendship. Maybe we are Lucy and Ethel.

"Piper, I didn't think I'd see you. Did you get my note?" Cam is standing next to me.

"Oh, Cam, I'm sorry, I was a million miles away, and you made me jump!"

"Well, I hope wherever you were, I was there with you," Cam says as he kisses my cheek. "I'll tell you what the note says. I called my sister, and my brother is out of prison, so it's all looking like it may be him. I'm meeting one of the officers now, and we're going to the hermit's house so the police can get a verification that I rode by yesterday. Then I've got a new shipment of plants coming in, so I'll be out and about until late. Will you be okay?"

"Yes, I've got some painting to catch up on, and then I'm seeing Sister Mary-Margaret tonight for *I Love Lucy*, so don't worry about me. Should we be worried with your brother somewhere? Do they think he's still here?"

"They have no idea. All the officers are looking for him, but he's no dummy. He's managed to lay low this whole time, so I'm sure he's not going to intentionally let himself be seen right now. My sister said he is quite a hardened person from his time in prison, but she thinks he had a love interest, so it's possible he's doing this for her. I want to try to believe something good about him, but it's not looking that way. So, be careful. I really don't think it has anything to do with you other than once you knew me, he wanted to make me look bad. Make sure you call a taxi to come home tonight. I would pick you up, but I'm not sure where I'll be. Just be safe. Someone you know is crazy about you," Cam says as he kisses me, this time on the lips.

"Okay, Mr. Red, you better keep it professional here on the grounds. You please be safe too. He is after you," I say, squeezing his hand.

"Happy painting!" Cam says as he heads down the porch steps. Christopher Columbus, but he's handsome!

I've started setting the small alarm clock that comes with the room when I paint, or I won't keep any of my appointments. I get lost in how the colors flow together and move on their own, making curves and edges I never intended but end up loving. My painting area and the view from my room are ideal. I wish I could have a little studio here, but maybe I can set something up at my new store. If I stay. When I stay. I don't know, there's still too much to consider.

The alarm goes off, giving me enough time to wolf down the sandwich I had brought up to my room and start the walk to see Sister Mary-Margaret. Once again, the Straits of Mackinac are working their magic. I'm feeling remarkably healed by the beauty that surrounds me. This little perfect place on the map that most people have no idea about is beyond words, and yet, here I am. It's all quite amazing. Thank you, God.

In our conversation last week Mary-Margaret challenged me with something I know I must face, but I didn't want to. If I believe what the Bible says, she said, I don't get to be the exception. I need to forgive, and that means forgiving my father. She pointed out that even if he doesn't deserve to be forgiven, I need to forgive because none of us deserve forgiveness. I don't deserve it, and yet I was forgiven, Jesus forgave me. It's becoming clear I'm not going to be able to forgive based on a feeling, because that's not happening. Just the thought of what my dad did, how he wrecked our family's life, and probably others, I want to think that he is paying an eternal price. I have much more praying and reading to do to understand more fully, but the fact that I am called to forgive is clear. There is no way I can confront my dad and see him be sorry for what he did; it's too late for that. And if I hate what he did, I can only imagine what Jesus felt about the way my dad ended up using the pulpit for his own gain. Sister Mary-Margaret gently told me that she knew it was a big problem in my moving forward in life. She reminded me that Paul was once Saul, a Christian killer. And David was an adulterer and a murderer.

140

"Even if you forgive, out of obedience alone, without the feelings, you need to accomplish this," she said.

The more I thought about what she said, the more I understood that my refusal to forgive was not doing damage to my dad, but to me.

"There's got to be a reason that they put that detail in the Bible, Jesus forgave the very people nailing Him to the cross. Unforgiveness causes damage," she said.

When I got back to my room that night after our time together and looked in the mirror in my beautiful bathroom in one of the best hotels in the world, what did I see? A very damaged human being, and I knew it was time to change. Walking out on my balcony I just started to cry and stare at the stars over the Straits of Mackinac. A big, beautiful world. And me, a peon. A damaged peon wasting precious life hating a person. So, I forgave my dad. I told Jesus, I don't know if that's how it's done, and I realize I may have to say this a million times when the thoughts of what happened come into my head, but I see this is the right way, and I want it. I forgive my dad. I asked the Lord to take away these horrible bitter feelings and thoughts I have toward him. I took myself out of the judge's chair, and I chose to leave it with the Lord. Whether he repented in that fiery death is not for me to decide. I left it all in His hands, and I forgave. I forgave because I am forgiven and we both know I didn't deserve it. I asked Jesus to help me to understand His ways so I can see more clearly the importance of always forgiving, no matter the situation. I can't wait to tell her that what she said really got me thinking, and that I have forgiven.

Our last visit meant everything to me, and here it is, time to be together again. I love the anticipation I feel ringing the rectory bell. Every visit with her is a treasure.

Hmm. Maybe she's got the TV turned up loudly or something, better ring again. She must have a different treat than we had planned, because I don't smell popcorn like I usually do. Oh, good, finally, footsteps.

"Yes, may I help you?" A nun I don't recognize cracks the door and peeks out at me.

"Uh, yes, where is Sister Mary-Margaret?" I ask. I don't like this. I saw her a week ago and everything was fine.

"Are you Piper?" she asks.

"Yes, is Sister Mary-Margaret okay?" I ask.

"Please come in. She told me you would be coming, and she left a message for you," she says. "I'm sorry, I'm Sister Gabriella. I'm covering for Sister Mary-Margaret because she got the call she's been waiting for, for a very long time."

"The call?" I say, feeling sad and scared. I really wanted to see her.

"Yes, she's been waiting to get the call to go to Kenya, Africa. It was always a possibility, but she's had so many delays. She's going to Kibera, to the slums, to work with a cholera and typhoid outbreak. The notice came and she only had a few hours to prepare and leave. She did mention to me that this might be a bit shocking for you as you hadn't talked about this possibility. This note will explain it, she said, and to let you know that she will write to you here on the island when she can. In the meantime, you are in her prayers daily, and she wants you to pray for her too. I'm sure there is much more in her note, but that is all she had time to say before she had to be on her way to meet all her transportation," Sister Gabriella says.

"I am shocked, I had no idea she was even thinking of going!" I say, my heart pounding and a shiver running down my spine at the news. I try to stop the tears that are coming.

"Well, she didn't talk about it much because she had been postponed so many times, I think she had given up on it, but it has been her heart's desire for a long time. It's one of the original reasons she became a nun, to serve the poor in Africa. So now, she is realizing her dream. I'm sorry, I understood that you watched *I Love Lucy* every week, but I'm not a fan. Would you like a cup of tea?" Sister Gabriella asks.

"No, thank you, that's very kind. I'm sure you have much to do to get settled. If you do get to talk to her or can send a word somehow, please tell her thank you. She has helped me so much and I will miss her terribly. I wish you all the best in your time here. It's a special place, that's for sure," I say heading for the door. My words tumble out in a rush, and I'm seeing through a blur as I blink fast to keep tears at bay.

"I'm here temporarily until the new nun comes to fill her place. Well, if we can ever be of service here, let me know. Bless you and good night."

Sister Gabriella closes the door behind me, and I couldn't be more shocked. Africa? Cholera and typhoid? Will she be in danger of catching those things and dying? I wonder why she never said anything, but maybe with my Africa story, she was hesitant to bring it up. Plus, we spent a lot of time talking about me and Lucy and Ethel of course. It's just like her to be thinking of others, and not herself.

There's just enough daylight left to read her letter. Walking down to the harbor across the street from St. Anne's I want to tuck myself into a small bench on the dock and be alone with her note. Even though I've only known Mary-Margaret for a short time, she feels like family to me. I'm happy that she is realizing her dream, but I had so much more I wanted to say to her, and so much more I know that she could teach me. And Africa—why of all the joints in the world, to paraphrase Bogey, did she have to choose that place, the very spot that has such a heart-wrenching memory for me? This feels like something has come full circle, except the circle has me trapped inside.

Opening the letter, I recognize the beautiful handwriting done with a fountain pen.

Dear Piper,

I know this is an abrupt way to leave, and I'm so sorry I didn't get to see you in person. I imagine right now that you're feeling a bit like Sister Mary Benedict in The Bells of St. Mary's, *when Father O'Malley sends her away and she can't understand it. But we as movie watchers know, there is a bigger purpose going on. I never thought I would be on the island this long, so the fact that I was here to get to know you I think was part of God's plan for me to wait. He always knows so much more than we do about the big picture, because I wouldn't have missed getting to know you for the world! What a delight you are, and how much fun we've had talking about movies and watching our I Love Lucy together! I doubt that I will catch any episodes where I'm headed, but I will remember the moments we sat and laughed and play them repeatedly in my mind.*

You have lived through a lot, Piper, but remember, there's a bigger picture and a plan for your life. My prayer for you is that you will get to know the Trinity, really know them, and live your life fulfilling all that was planned for you since the beginning of time. I know that it has been my destiny to go to Africa when the time was right, so I hope you won't feel sad that I am gone. I leave you with the Word of God. If I end up having an address and am reachable at some point, I will try to contact you on the island. Lord willing, we will reconnect at some point, and if not here, then in eternity. That's all very serious stuff for two ladies who love to laugh and enjoy I Love Lucy! Goodbye for now as my time is so short until my boat leaves. I know with all my heart that Jesus is The Way, The Truth, and The Life, and when someone gives their life to Him, they will have the peace and direction needed to live an abundant life of love and joy, no matter the circumstances. That is my prayer and wish for you, my dear friend.

Your friend always,

Sister Mary-Margaret

The waves are lapping up against the sides of the multiple boats in the harbor and it's a soothing sound. Change seems to be the norm in my life lately. Closing the letter as night envelopes me, I do feel sadness at the thought of not seeing her for a long time, but also a peace. I think I am understanding that she was an answer to prayer for me, to help me get back on the right path, and in a way that I would listen. It's such a quiet evening and in the corner of the bench in the dark, I feel like I'm a part of the air. No one can see me, and I can see everything.

Darn, there's a couple coming up out of the bottom of their boat, which is disturbing my pristine silence.

"You stop it, Dotty." The guy is tickling her.

With the quiet and the shape of the harbor, their voices echo like they are talking on microphones.

"No, you stop it, Chad. Hey, is this stupid thing going to work?" the girl says back.

"I think I can get it started. Something's not quite right, but it should get us at least out of here," he says.

Her voice sounds so familiar. Maybe it's one of the tourists I saw on the porch who arrived here on a boat. I'll take out my binoculars; I need a closer look. A little adjustment to compensate for the dusk and there. Are you kidding? That's why she sounds familiar. It's Miss Fields! Finally, I know her first name—Dotty. And she has a boyfriend, that's interesting. Let's get a closer look at this guy Chad she's been dating, and then I will get back to my own business.

I'm becoming a busybody! Come on, turn around. Tall, dark, and handsome? No, he's tall, with red hair. Red hair? What? This must be Cam's brother! Even though it's quite murky from this far away, I swear I saw red hair. Cam did say all their names started with a *C* so that would add up too. But why is he with Miss Fields? I try to be as quiet as possible and grab my satchel. I need to get a little closer to the pier where their boat is tied up. I don't know if I should go and get help first or confront them. I think the guy had red hair. Maybe if I can get a closer look and not be seen, I would have some idea. If I'm wrong, I don't want to cause a scene. I'll just creep along and... No! Ouch, that was a bad turn on my ankle and a terrible fall, I couldn't even stop the impact with my hands. Oh, my ankle, and yes, that is my own voice screaming in pain!

"Who's there? Chad, someone is on this pier, go see who it is!" Dotty is looking in my direction.

I can't get up because of the pain, even with all my effort. I can't put any weight on my foot. Chad is getting closer, but I can't run away. Oh my gosh, he does have red hair and he does resemble Cam a bit. Except, I've never seen such a mean look on Cam's face. This is not good.

"Help! Call the Police!" At least I have the good sense to start yelling despite the pain. I have to yell; I think this guy is going to do something to me. "Help! Help! Help!"

"Shut her up or something!" Dotty yells to Chad.

"I can't shut her up and I see someone else coming. We've got to get out of here." Chad tries to yell louder than me.

"Oh my gosh, that's Piper Penn! Grab her, she's going to have to come with us. She knows who I am," Dotty yells.

Chad grabs my arms and he's dragging me down the pier toward their boat! I feel every bump and splinter as it lodges in my already painful leg. Rolling me on the boat, he lets me fall from the edge to the floor. Thud!

"Help me, help!" I just keep screaming the best I can.

"Shut up! Shut up!" Chad yells back at me.

"Piper, if you know what's good for you, you'll shut up!" Dotty says.

Out of the corner of my eye, I see some commotion by the guy I was yelling toward on the other pier in the distance, so I can only hope he's calling for help.

"Dotty Fields, what are you doing? I've hurt myself, and I don't want to be on this boat. Help me! Why are you here? This is the guy who robbed the bank, the guy you saw coming out. Don't tell me you were in on this too," I say.

"Quit being so nosy, Piper," she says as she plasters a piece of duct tape over my mouth. "If you weren't such an inquisitive girl, we would be on our way, and you wouldn't know a thing about this. I tried to keep you out of all of it, but here you are, throwing yourself in the mix. You're stupid, that's what you are," she adds, tying my hands behind my back.

My ankle is throbbing, but I'm trying to put some mind over matter and keep my head about me, because I don't know how bad these people are. Would they really hurt me? A glance at my ankle tells me I've never seen swelling like that, and I see little blobs of blood and scrapes all over my legs.

"Quick, get the anchor in, we're taking off!" Chad yells at Dotty.

Dotty untethers the boat and Chad gets the motor going. With such loud chugging, it must be operating poorly; there is some kind of problem. Thank goodness, it might give me a chance.

"We can't go fast, but at least we can get out of here, and if we have to, this idiot will be our bargaining chip," Chad says to Dotty.

"Her name is Piper Penn and word has it she's dating your brother!" Dotty says.

"Oh really, the high and mighty Cam? How is the wonder boy who does everything right? Well isn't that interesting that I would have control over his girlfriend. Hmm, this is very interesting. Maybe I can get back at him even more than I had hoped," Chad says as the boat starts to unevenly chug forward.

"Well, Miss Penn, now you have met *my* boyfriend. I've been in love with him ever since we started writing after I intercepted his letter to Mr. Sawyer looking for a lawyer. I've been trying to get off this stupid island for most of my life. After that first visit to see this handsome redhead in prison, I had no doubt he would be my ticket out. Seems we both enjoy the sight of a handsome redhead, huh? My guy knows how to get money, real money, and have a good time. Right, sweetie pie?" Dotty says, winking at Chad. "My man and I even made a trip to San Francisco to try to check you out, but that guy at the movie theatre was no help, and we had to get back. I was trying to see if we could use your inheritance somehow, and during that trip is when I hatched this, if I do say so myself, brilliant plot to rob the bank. Yes, I think 'brilliant' describes it perfectly. Burning down your building provided the perfect distraction. And I did make sure you had extra fire insurance, so you're welcome. It was the perfect plan with the perfect outcome, right sweetie?"

"Yah, all except for this piece of crap boat which isn't going to get us out of here fast enough," he yells back to Dotty.

If this wasn't really all happening before my eyes, I might think I'm stuck in some B-movie with Dotty Fields playing the cheesy gangster's moll. But, it's all too real, and now I know who was checking me out in San Fran. I can't yell anymore with this freaking tape on my mouth, but that commotion in the distance could be someone trying to help me, at least I hope so.

Lord, I need protection. The pain is getting as intense as the swelling I feel in my ankle, and I think this light-headedness must be the thing that happens before fainting. I'm scared.

"Crap, your yelling got them stirred up. I think they're coming after us," Chad shouts at me. "Grab something to hit her with if we need to, Dotty. She's going to be our ticket out of here.".

"Hit her? I'd rather not, but I will if I have to. Here, how about this baseball bat? That should work if I need it," Dotty says.

With great difficulty, I push myself up into a corner so I can at least see what's happening outside of the boat. Oh my gosh! A boat is coming full speed at us and it doesn't look like Chad can outrun them with the sputtering sounds from this piece of junk which is failing more by the minute. Someone on the approaching boat is talking with a megaphone, and I'm so thankful they are getting closer.

"This is the Coast Guard. Cut your engine. I repeat, cut your engine now or face the consequences."

"What are we going to do, Chad?" Dotty screams while picking up the bat and moving closer toward me.

"They better let us go, or the chick is going to get it," Chad screams.

"I repeat, cut your engine, or face the consequences. This is your last warning," the voice on the megaphone is talking louder.

Chad cuts the engine but moves closer to me. He yanks me up by my hair as a spotlight lights up our boat. Now my head hurts as much as my ankle.

"Do anything and this chick is going to get a bat to the head," Chad yells in the direction of the spotlight.

"Calm down, sir, no one needs to get hurt," the voice replies, sounding like someone trying to keep calm himself.

"If you don't want to witness a bat to the head, you better let us be on our way," Chad yells at the voice.

"Sir, bat or no bat, you're not going to be able to get away. Your boat isn't working, and either way, you're going to be overcome, so save yourself some serious extra charges, and stop all of this right now," the voice says firmly.

"Chad, I don't want to go to jail. Maybe we should just stop now," Dotty cries frantically. It seems the severity of what's happening might be finally hitting her, too.

"Shut up, Dotty, I know what I'm doing," Chad screams at her and turns his attention to the Coast Guard boat. "I want a fast boat brought here and I want it now. If you don't want to see two chicks die before your eyes, then you'll get me that boat."

"Sir, calm down. No one needs to get hurt." The voice is remaining calm as Chad's voice is ratcheting up in intensity.

"Chad, what do you mean two chicks? You mean me too?" Dotty screams at him.

"I'm not going back to prison, no way. I'm getting out of here, whatever it takes," Chad screams back.

"You creep! After all I did for you, making it easy to rob the bank!

And what about the jewels? You think you had any hand in that? They were all my ideas. I did all the real work. All you did was walk in and out of a bank, I did all the planning, the waiting. You rat! You said you loved me, you said we'd get married. You dirt bag!"

Dotty's face is red, and she is getting louder and louder. The last thing I remember is seeing the bat coming toward me and throwing my head back in an effort to miss it.

Chapter Twenty

Waking up to smelling salts, I have several paramedics hovering over me, and I'm back on the shore by the piers in a gurney, unless I'm dreaming? No, this is real, I hear lots of people talking around me. What happened? Everything stings and oh, my ankle. Wait, it's coming back. I was captive on the boat and Dotty was about to slam a bat into my head.

"What happened? How did I get here?" I want to raise my head, but the dizziness forces me back down. And the pain in my leg... man, this hurts.

"Just lie still, ma'am," the man above me says as he gently pats my shoulder. Okay, I may have been knocked out, but I still remember I hate to be called "ma'am".

"From what the Coast Guard captain said, you hit your head when you threw it back to miss the bat. The lady who hit you wasn't really aiming for you, she was just winding up to really let the guy have a good whack to the head," the paramedic says.

"Oh my gosh, Dotty hit Chad instead of me?" I ask.

"Yes, she really gave him a good one, knocked him out. That allowed the Coast Guard to board and take control of the situation. The police already have those two in custody and will be transferring them to the mainland shortly for prosecution. Looks like you escaped a tragedy," he says.

Even with all this pain, I'm thankful to be alive and to finally have this whole mess of a robbery over with. *Thank you, Lord.*

"Piper! Piper!" Cam is running down the sidewalk toward me. "Piper, I got here as fast I could. Oh my gosh, what can I do to help?" he asks the paramedic.

"We're going to have her sit up in a minute and see how she does. It's a small concussion, and a badly bruised ankle. Unfortunately, they hurt worse than a break. I'm getting a list of the things to watch for like headache, blurred vision, or extreme weakness. If any of that happens, call emergency right away," the paramedic says.

He goes on with instructions to Cam about icing my ankle, no straining my eyes, and a lot of other stuff that is sounding blurry in my head right now. Cam looks like he's catching all of this. Wait, what's this about going to the hospital on the mainland?

"No, I'll be okay. I'll follow your instructions and we can take it from here. Thank you, I'm feeling better now," I say.

I'm not really feeling better, but I don't want to leave the island. I just want to go back to my room. That will help, I know it.

"Thank you, guys, I'll take care of her, I'll make sure if there's any problems she gets the help she needs," Cam says, stroking my hair.

As the paramedics head back to their equipment and start to pick things up, I see the familiar face of the island police officers.

"So, we'll need a statement from you, Piper, but I think it's safe to say, Cam, that you are cleared of all charges. What we now know is that your brother came here right after getting out of prison and has been laying low thanks to Dotty Fields help. She had been writing letters and even visiting him downstate while he was incarcerated. They hatched up this scheme to rob the bank, and the fire at your place, Piper, was a distraction so they could carry out the robbery undisturbed. Because we don't have much of that kind of crime here, they saw it all as an easy target," the officer says.

"That's what I thought might have happened. What in the world got into Chad's head? I guess I have no idea what goes on in prison," Cam says.

"Obviously we have to do better than we have when it comes to these types of things," the officer continues. "And, we solved another crime—who stole the jewelry from the movie set. That was Dotty Fields too. She told us everything when we caught them. Being mad at Chad really helped. As they say, hell hath no fury like a woman scorned."

"Yah, she turned on him pretty fast when he offered to throw her into the mix of getting whacked with a bat if he could get a fast boat for a getaway. Thank goodness she has a temper and went ballistic or I really don't know what would have happened to me. I think Chad would have hit me. It was terrifying. And, Cam, he did not say nice things about you. I think he has nursed these feelings about you in prison and it made him a very bitter person. Not only did he want the money, he wanted to hurt you in the process," I say.

"It's so sad. I'm so relieved you are okay, but I feel bad that my brother caused all this," Cam says, a tremble in his voice. He turns his head away. "I'm also ashamed that I didn't realize what he was turning into these last few years. I should have tried to visit him and maybe it wouldn't have come to this."

"What's done is done. Maybe you can see about requesting some help for him in prison from a counselor or something once the dust all settles. Knowing that you care for him may start some healing. And, we can pray for him," I say softly.

"Yes, we can, and I'm so thankful you weren't hurt worse. I can't imagine what you've been through tonight," Cam says. "Do you feel up to going to the police station now?"

"Yes, Piper, if you can't, we understand," says the police officer, looking at me expectantly. "But it would be best if you could."

"I can make it. I want to get this all behind me. I want to wake up tomorrow and feel like it's a new day," I say.

Cam helps me into a horse taxi, as I balance the crutches the paramedic gave me, and we head for the police station. Having his arm around me while I answer questions and fill out paperwork makes me feel much calmer. I put my head on his shoulder as we take the taxi back up to the Grand. The rhythmic clip-clop of the horses soothes my head. Neither of us speak on the ride back. I think he senses I need to be quiet for a moment. Helping me up the stairs to the porch, he leads me inside toward the elevator.

"Listen, Piper, I know it's not quite appropriate, but I don't want to leave you alone tonight because of the instruction sheet I got about the concussion. So, you go to bed, and I'll be out on the balcony in the lounge chair. That way I can check on you, and if you need something I'll be right here," Cam says.

"I'm not gonna argue, Dr. Cam, I think it will make me feel better knowing you are checking on me. Thank goodness they had crutches for me," I say.

"We have so, so much to talk about, Piper. But I think tonight, we will let it all go. You get ready for bed. I'll be out on the balcony and call me when you're ready. I'm going to tuck you in with a kiss and a prayer. It's time to sleep and recuperate. We'll tackle life tomorrow. It will still all be here. But tonight, rest. How does that sound?" Cam asks holding open the door for me into my room. "Will you be able to get ready for bed by yourself?"

"You, sir, have made an excellent plan. I am exhausted, but I can manage. I do need to bring everything down a notch. What a day. I didn't even tell you that Sister Mary-Margaret is gone, she's going to Africa," I say.

"Africa? What in the world… but, wait, like I said, so, so much to talk about. But, not tonight. Bedtime, my love," Cam says tenderly.

He heads for the balcony and I hobble to the bathroom. Everything will have to wait until tomorrow. What a day it will be.

Chapter Twenty-One

In all the hubbub of the last few days, I zoned out the fact the movie was wrapping up production, at least as far as anything that concerned the extras. Perfect timing because I couldn't live up to my maid skills anyway. I missed the chance to dress up for a big dining room scene, but the assistant director understood. They were happy to get their jewelry back, which they found in Dotty's apartment. Laying low in my room for a few days and only staying up to eat and touch base with Cam, I had taken his advice to heart. I didn't have a choice. My body pretty much shut down. Cam and I didn't talk at all about what happened, but instead spoke only of the weather and the good food. We know how to read each other's needs. It's sweet. But now I think I'm finally ready to do some processing of everything that has happened and to think about what is next. I'm even going to get dressed like a real girl and meet Cam for lunch in the dining hall. He's reserved a table right by the window in the corner, so we'll have some privacy, and a gorgeous view.

It's been good to get my strength back, and I've also had some time to do some real prayer and reflection in my half-sleep, half-awake state. I know that Jesus has been with me through all of this, protecting me, and ultimately saving my life. Both ways—on the boat, and eternally. I have a very long way to go, but I do feel as though I've come a long way since I came to this island as a prickly, hurt, half-alive human with no faith, and no direction. I really wish I could tell all of this to Sister Mary-Margaret, but that will have to wait for another time. I'm hoping we get to connect with letters again.

My room smells like a flower garden with a daily delivery from Cam and an additional daily bouquet sent on behalf of Katherine. Being "in the know" of all things island, she must have been told that Cam had nothing to do with notes under her door, or stealing jewelry, or any of it. I'm sure Chad's behavior did nothing to put that family back into her good graces, but she should realize that Cam is innocent. I think the flowers are her way of saying to both of us that she was out of line. When I showed them to Cam, he just made a snorting sound and commented that they weren't as nice as the flowers he grew right on the grounds of the Grand. My sweet boy, we both have so much to learn about forgiveness. Plus, Katherine is still hoping I'll sell, so I can count on her kissing up to me if there's a chance she can get her prized property. As long as she needs something from me, she has to be civil.

Getting dressed today, I'm in the mood to look extra nice. A few more curls, my new bright mauve lipstick, and yes, one of these lovely flowers from Cam's bouquet does look good behind my ear. I told Cam I would meet him at the entrance to the dining room. With each step heading down toward the entrance I can't help but marvel once again at this lovely place. My free time here will be over soon. It has been purely magical to walk these beautiful hallways every day, sit on the magnificent porch, be a part of a movie that I hope will be successful, and just be a part of the Grand family.

And there he is, Mr. Red, my boyfriend, I guess. Funny, I never thought of that word in my vocabulary. Mr. Boyfriend. I like the sound of it.

"Hey, beautiful, you look lovely. I like the flower." There he is. So handsome and waiting for me.

"Well, thank you, sir, I happen to know the gardener, and he is one talented guy. It feels really good to walk instead of hobble along, too." I've been able to chuck the crutches, since my ankle is healing nicely. Taking my hand, he walks with me to the table set aside for us. It's just the way he described it, in the corner, by the window and quite private. Holding out my chair, my wonderful waiter gives me a smile and says: "Milady." Ah, I'm going to miss that too.

After settling on iced tea to start, and returning from the luncheon buffet, which seems to go on for miles, we dive into scrumptious delicacies as only the Grand can make them, as beautiful as they are delicious.

"So, how are you? Ankle back to normal? Any signs of concussion problems? You seem to be doing well. I was a little worried because you wanted to sleep, but I think you were just worn out from something so traumatic," Cam says.

"Whoa, so many questions! I think you're right. The whole ordeal wore me out, and the bonk on the head didn't help. I'm pretty sure there's no lasting damage, but you can be the judge of that. My ankle is still sore, but it is mending quickly. I'm not ready for a marathon, but I'm amazed how fast it is getting better."

"And how's your heart?"

This man. What a question.

"My heart is happy and sad at the same time. So happy that this is over, but not that it's your brother, and there are so many lives in a mess. I've gone down that wrong road, so I have no business judging anyone, that's for sure. They're young, there can be some redemption along the way. I hope they find faith, Jesus, and the right path. Without it, I think we're all kind of headed the wrong way, even if we look good on the outside. Never thought in a million years I'd hear myself say anything like that, but I believe it now," I say.

"I want you to know that I spoke to the Conrad brothers, and they were very encouraging about the cleanup and remodel. They think they can salvage a lot, and only extend the build by a month or so. I'm sure once you explore what the insurance pays for, it should cover the costs to get someone from the mainland in who specializes in cleaning up smoke damage. You don't want to have to deal with that. And, come to find out, it was Dotty was the one who took out extra insurance. She must have felt guilty about her plan to burn down your place. Mr. Sawyer isn't sure how that will all pan out, but there's a possibility you will get more. Even if you don't, the initial insurance will cover the cost, and you're not in any trouble," Cam says.

"Wow, thanks so much for checking into that for me. That's good news. She did say something about that when she was screaming at me on the boat, but I don't remember everything she said. I was thinking that since my time here is almost up, I'll just find a small room to rent until I can at least live in the apartment above the store. They can make that the priority so I can have a place to stay."

"So, I have some questions for you. First one, are you thinking of staying on the island, I mean long-term?"

"That's a big question! I have been praying to see what I should do, and Freddy comes to mind. He's not related to me, but then who is anymore?"

"Good one, Piper." He takes on the voice of an emcee to gently mock me: "She's here all week folks!" And then he leans in. "At least your sense of humor is intact!"

"Thanks! But really, I am thinking of Freddy. I have to at least offer to bring him here and set him up in some kind of senior living. I did a little checking and there's a shared home for seniors that would offer him some companionship, even if he drives them crazy! I don't know how he would handle the winters here, and I don't know how I will manage them either, but he's not much of an outdoorsman anyway. If there are people there who want to hear a lot of stories, he will be fine. Of course, I'll plan on seeing him too. He may not want to come, but I think he will, and I want to offer. So that's a long answer to say, I need to do right by Freddy, and then, yes, I believe my life is here. I think I can turn my shop into a small gallery of sorts for my artwork, and make it work. Selling my art in the shop here was a good test to see if people would buy it, and it seems they would. Maybe a small coffee shop and a place people can play music too. I've got some ideas."

"That sounds like a plan that would fit in very well downtown. There's nothing like that, and with the tourist season getting bigger every year, what you do could be a very big hit. That leads me to my next question," Cam says with a smile.

Out of the corner of my eye, I see the waiters are gathering around us, and they're humming. Wait. What's happening? They're getting closer and closer, and everyone is looking at me. I turn back to Cam and he isn't in his chair anymore. He is down on one knee in front of me and I feel his hand take mine.

"My next question, Miss Piper Penn, is this, one of the most important questions of my life. Will you do me the honor of becoming my wife? Will you marry me?" Cam asks.

"Oh my gosh, Cam. I did not know this was coming... I'm so touched." I can't believe this is happening!

"Is that a yes?"

"Yes, yes, a thousand times yes!"

We both stand up and I give him the biggest hug, and a very modest kiss because of where we are. All the waiters are clapping and smiling, as are many fellow diners. From boyfriend to fiancé in a matter of minutes. This is kind of crazy, but good crazy! Everyone says something sweet and I can't stop looking at the little diamond ring on my hand. It's a perfect circle and the light from the window makes it sparkle.

"Do you like it? I popped over to Mackinaw City one morning and picked it out at a jewelry store there. It was hard to choose, but I thought it would be something that you would like."

"I love it, Cam. It's perfect."

"I know it's not a Hollywood-size diamond, but it's real."

"Are you kidding? We'll leave those kinds of diamonds, and the price tag that goes with them, to Elizabeth Taylor. This is more than I could have ever imagined. And it's a gorgeous sentiment, but it's the meaning behind it that is everything to me. The man behind it that is everything to me."

"I love you, Piper, with all my heart. I know we haven't dated a long time, but I know you are the one. I think I knew it right away. And, I prayed, I did. I told God I was willing to set my own feelings aside, if it wasn't His will, but I think you came to the island for us to start a new life together."

"I love you, Cam. I think you're right. It's a new beginning and boy do I need that. "

"I'm hoping we'll be married soon, and you won't have to rent a place at all. We can live in my grounds house, and then you can decide what you want to do with your place. We can go there, or you could rent it out… or possibly set it up for Freddy. We'll have lots of options. I'm thinking we could have a small wedding right here at the Grand Hotel, and I know they will help us with a wedding supper. I could invite my sister, but other than that, I don't have family, and I'm not sure if there are people outside of the island you would invite?"

"You've thought of everything! Freddy is all I have left in San Francisco. I wish Sister Mary-Margaret could be here, but that's not possible. Very small and quiet is good with me. I just want us to be together, and wow, I can't even wrap my head around the word 'Mrs.' yet! I love the idea. I love you."

"Piper Nelson. Mr. and Mrs. The sooner, the better I say. I can't wait to be husband and wife."

"Um, there is something I haven't told you about myself. It is something that you're going to learn if I don't tell you, so I'd rather you know about it ahead of time. I can't believe I'm going to have to tell you this, but it has become a necessity."

Cam looks worried. I hope my wink reassures him.

Chapter Twenty-Two

I don't know who thought of it first, but the minute it was mentioned, we both knew it was right. The place for us to get married was the center of the labyrinth below the Grand Hotel. Cam set up a time for us to talk to the pastor of the Little Stone Church just down the lane from the Grand, and he agreed to do the ceremony. It had become our Sunday morning church and a place to learn more about the Bible. We are both hungry to know more and grow as Christians. After all my dreaming about Hollywood, this is better. Real life is better than any movie. I know I'll always love movies, but now they are just a way to be entertained. I think my days of writing to movie stars for peace and reflection are over. I've found something so much better—the Father, the Son, and the Holy Spirit will be my Guides and my Comforters.

Picking a Saturday morning, our small group gathers for this very important moment in the lives of Cam and I—the ceremony where we pledge our lives to one another.

"Funny thing about labyrinths," Freddy says.

"Oh Freddy, I just knew we could count on you for facts about labyrinths!" I say.

Yes, the FredMeister is making a name for himself on the island. With a little weight loss and the fact that he has decided to eat right and take better care of himself, Freddy is doing quite well and seems to have easily settled into island life. Holding onto his arm as we are partly hidden in the woods as the ceremony is about to begin, I'm so glad he is here to walk me over to Cam.

"In fact, in Germany, young men would walk through a labyrinth as part of their initiation into adulthood," Freddy concludes.

"Fredrick, you never cease to amaze me, but right now, we have a job to get done. Time to bring me to the center for a very important ceremony. And, Freddy, I'm so happy you are here with me."

Wiping a tear and looking away for a moment, I hear the trembling in his voice.

"Pip, you have no idea what it means to me, to be here right now, and I just know your family is here with us too. That's something I don't know about, but I believe there is happiness for you and your future with Mr. Cam. I was so lost after you left San Francisco, and I thought there was no reason to go on. You bringing me here has meant the world to me. I feel twenty years younger and life seems so good. Thank you for not giving up on me."

"Freddy, you were always in my heart, and I'm sorry it took me so long to understand how much we needed each other. I wasted some years there, and I wasn't very nice to you, and you stood by me. Do you forgive me?"

"I only have thankfulness that we could help each other through some very hard days. And now I want only the best for you and your almost-husband. Are you ready, sweet girl? This is one of the best moments of my life too. I know you will have a happily-ever-after with Cam and living on this island."

As we start the walk around the trees and to the labyrinth circle, I see Cam, and my heart is bursting with love. It's just a few of our friends and the pastor, and I thank you Lord for making all this possible. You have given me gifts beyond my wildest imagination, and I love you, Lord. Thank you for not giving up on me. Thank you that you took the greatest tragedy I could imagine, and you worked it together for good. Thank you for saving me, and Cam. My prayer is that we will be lights for you on this island.

I let go of Freddy's arm when we reach the center and turn to Cam's face. The look in his eyes makes my heart leap. It's a feeling of pure joy that we have found each other. After each saying a few words from our hearts, the pastor tells us, from Ecclesiastes chapter four and verse twelve, how a triple-braided cord is not easily broken, and even though we have each other, that third cord is Jesus. I want to remember that.

"I now pronounce you man and wife," the pastor says.

"Give her a big kiss, Mr. Cam! She's your wife now!" Freddy does a little jump of glee.

"Good idea, Fredrick!" Cam says.

And with that, I receive a very stunning kiss from the redhead as a married lady!

"One formality before we head up to the dining room for our brunch, Mr. and Mrs. Nelson. I need you to sign the marriage license to make it truly official," the pastor says as he pulls out the papers with a pen and places them on the bench at the outside of the labyrinth.

"Cam, you sign here. Please sign your official name, Cameron Raymond Nelson."

"Gladly!" Cam says as he signs.

"And now, Piper..." the pastor says.

"That's actually not my first name, and if you look closely, you will see it. I am happy to sign my full real name," I say.

Reaching for the pen, I stand for a moment and catch the sunlight peeking through the trees and shining on us in the labyrinth. I take a deep breath, a happy breath of thankfulness. I bend over to sign my full name.

Mrs. Ethel Piper Nelson.

The End

A Note to You...

Dear Reader,

I hope reading *Being Ethel (In a world that loves Lucy)* enriched your journey! If you've never been to Mackinac Island, it's glorious. If you have been to the island, or perhaps this was your read on a vacation—that sounds marvelous. *Being Ethel* was born out of my love of everything *I Love Lucy* and Mackinac Island. My husband and I have visited for over thirty years, and the magic is always there.

My hope is that this book encourages you to take a closer look at your own faith walk and the joy and abundant life that awaits anyone who chooses Jesus as Savior. It's a free gift, available to anyone, anytime. There's a forever family that awaits each of us with a call to magnificent love.

Being Ethel (In a World That Loves Lucy) is the first book in a trilogy set on Mackinac Island. Together, we will travel and learn through the art of story, a creative gift we can share.

Meanwhile, please enjoy the beginning lines of my next novel—*Being Dorothy (In a world longing for home)*

Please stay in touch for the latest news and sometimes a giveaway!

I love to hear from readers! info@lakegirlpublishing.com

My heartfelt thanks,

Michèle

Chapter One

Being Dorothy

(In a world longing for home)

1980

His shadow in the corner is not what I expected. I can't believe he found me here in Vienna.

"Let's go." His voice sounds almost threatening, and I'm not sure what to make of this.

I'm sure he loves that I dropped my book when I noticed him. I can't let him see that his presence is affecting my breathing. Seeing him in the corner of the room is surreal, it's finally happened. The other shoe has dropped. I don't have the right word in my head right now for the combination of panic and pleasure overtaking me.

"It was our agreement, and I'm here, so let's go." Gideon's words and his intent gaze have rattled me, but I must take this back in my control. He can't see me as weak.

"Gideon, I can't believe you're here. How did you get in my suite?" Good. That sounded controlled and calm, just what I was hoping for.

"I've got friends at the Sacher Hotel too, Dorothy. I spent a few years in Vienna, remember?" he says.

Dorothy, huh? No 'Dee Dee'? Just 'Dorothy'. This means he's not happy about this moment. I can't stop staring at him. I still can't believe he found me.

"Let's go," he says. Still keeping it mater-of-fact huh, Gideon? You are a pro at hiding all emotions. I guess some things never change.

"Are you going to hurt me?" I ask. I can stare too, mister. I can give it right back.

"You know I would never hurt you," Gideon says with a slight crack in his tone, but his eyes never leave my face.

"Are you going to force me?" I ask. Come on, Gideon, show something I can read on your face. What are your intentions here?

"If I have to, I will. I'd prefer not to. You have to live up to your end of the agreement," he says.

I jump as two men even farther back in the shadows step forward. Oh, so he's come prepared.

"What if things are different now?" I ask.

Nice long pause, Gideon. Is that just for effect?

"What if they are? That doesn't change the agreement. Let's go."

He's waiting for me to move, I guess. I don't see a way out of this, especially with the extra guys he brought. At least he doesn't take my capabilities for granted. I wonder where I screwed up. I didn't think he would find me.

"I need my things, where are we going?" I ask.

I get up. He takes a step toward me now that I've moved.

"Your things will follow. Just get your purse and passport, we're going home. I have a jet," he says.

Oh, I see he has risen in his role, to now have jets at his disposal. Nice work if you can get it.

"Gideon, it's been almost a year. Maybe we should just have dinner and see how that goes," I say.

Maybe there's a way to slow this down.

"We're leaving right now. The jet is waiting for us. Get your purse and your passport. That's all you need for now. Let's go," he says. The broken record tactic. Continue to repeat your request. I know that one.

He takes another step closer to me, and his henchmen follow. There doesn't appear to be a way out of leaving with him.

"I really want to know how you found me. Did you bribe some staff?" I ask.

We're closer now and I look directly into those teal-blue eyes, the same eyes that used to give away his mood of the moment.

"All my years in The Service paid off, I guess, That's another story for another time. Right now, we must leave," he says with the slightest hint of a smile, the kind that shows satisfaction at winning.

"I guess my time with that wonderful organization didn't prepare me enough to outsmart you. I didn't get *your* special training," I say.

I need to stay snarky to keep control of this as much as I can. At least there's no training that allows him to see the million feelings and thoughts shooting through my brain.

"I was always going to find you. It was just a matter of time. The pilot is waiting, and some new circumstances have arisen that put us both in danger," he says. He's returned to a more somber tone. Just a matter of time, huh? Still so sure of yourself, aren't you Gideon?

With my purse in hand, I succumb. We're going to a place that only we know as our home, to people who have no idea about the life we've led. But what circumstances can be so dire that we have to hide in this place we've kept secret from everyone? Why don't I have knowledge of these "circumstances" he brings up? Could our ultimate fear be happening? Life is about to change, and going with this man, my husband, is the last thing I want to do.

Stay tuned for the release of Book 2 in *A Mackinac Island Story* series.

Being Dorothy
(In a world longing for home)
Michèle Olson
info@lakegirlpublishing.com

About the Author

Michèle Olson has an over-forty-year career in advertising and marketing as a writer in all mediums, with an emphasis in health writing. She has also enjoyed a professional voice career including time as a DJ (yes, even when they still played records!) and has voiced local to national commercials and voice projects.

It has always been her dream to segue into fiction and *Being Ethel (In a world that loves Lucy)* is the first in a series based on Mackinac Island—a tiny island in the Straits of Mackinac that connect the Upper and Lower Peninsula of Michigan. A visitor there along with her husband for over thirty years, she loves to tell people about this unique place with no cars and plenty of fudge!

A mom, a mother-in-love, and a "Gee Gee" (G as in good), Michèle resides with her husband in the shadow of Lambeau Field, where life around football abounds. She cherishes her faith and family above all and is delighted to take you on this trip to Mackinac Island, a place that has brought her so much respite and joy.

She loves connecting, so reach back through all the social media links provided. Next? It's a trip back to Mackinac in **Being Dorothy (In a world longing for home)**.

You can connect with me on:

- 🌐 https://www.lakegirlpublishing.com
- 🐦 https://twitter.com/modawnwriter
- ⓕ https://www.facebook.com/LakeGirlPublishing
- 🔗 https://www.instagram.com/lakegirlpublishing
- 🔗 https://www.linkedin.com/in/michele-olson-51bb202a

Subscribe to my newsletter:

- ✉️ https://www.lakegirlpublishing.com/copy-of-about-4

Made in the USA
Monee, IL
25 July 2024